I0788592

BEING THE SUUN

LEGENDS OF THE FALLEN BOOK 4

J.A. CULICAN

CASSIDY TAYLOR

ISBN-13: 978-1-949621-10-5

Dragon Realm Press

www.dragonrealmpress.com

❀ Created with Vellum

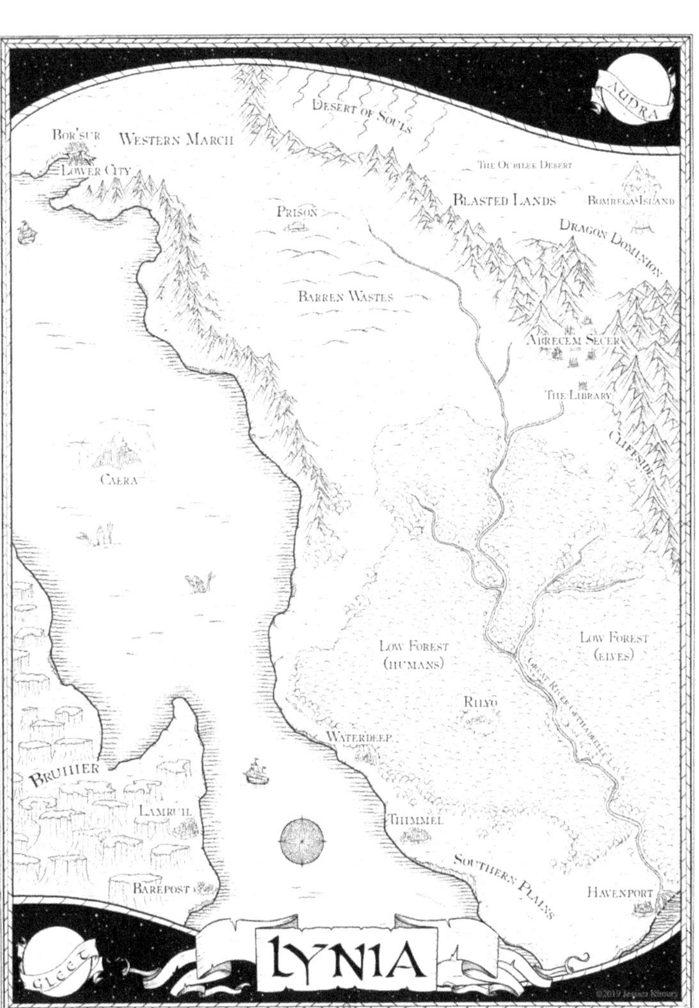

AUDRA
DESERT OF SOULS
BOR'SUR
WESTERN MARCH
LOWER CITY
THE OUBILEE DESERT
PRISON
BLASTED LANDS
BOMREGA ISLAND
DRAGON DOMINION
BARREN WASTES
ARRECEM SECER
THE LIBRARY
CLIFFSIDE
CAERA
LOW FOREST
(HUMANS)
LOW FOREST
(ELVES)
RILYO
GREAT RIVER OF THADRELL
WATERDEEP
BRUHIER
LAMRUIL
THIMMEL
SOUTHERN PLAINS
HAVENPORT
BAREPOST
GLEEC
LYNIA
©2019 Jacquza Khoury

CHAPTER 1

I caught the blazetaur's horn on the blade of my sword with a loud, echoing clash. Birds stirred from the nearby trees. Their little black bodies lifted into the mist and disappeared.

The beast heaved its weight against me.

I dug in my heels, a scream of effort rising in my throat. Its beady black eyes—too small for its face—seemed to laugh at me. I could see why in the image reflected back at me. My dirt-smeared face, torn leather vest, leaves in my short, yellow hair. Yeah. I was a real terrifying opponent.

"Frida!" Estrid's voice called across the clearing. She burst through the trees and ran toward me, stealing the blazetaur's attention.

It released me.

I fell forward, narrowly avoiding being trampled by one massive foot.

It swung its barbed tail in a wide arc, moving faster than any creature its size had a right to.

"I almost had him." I pushed myself to my feet and trailed

behind the monster, taking useless swings with my sword at its armored backside.

The poisonous barbed tail struck out at Estrid.

She ducked and rolled.

The stinger stabbed into the trunk of a tree with a thunderous crack and stuck there. The soft spot at the base of its stinger was the creature's only weak spot. Sever it, and the monster died. We'd learned that lesson the hard way in our three years on this blasted island.

Estrid rolled to a stop, covered in leaves and mud, and cursed. She would have preferred to be covered in blazetaur goo.

I reached her and grabbed her by the arm, pulling her to her feet.

The monster struggled to free itself from the tree, bellowing and thrashing about wildly. Its armored body slammed against nearby trees, cracking two of them in half.

"You found it." Erik, our big brother, emerged from the tree line across the clearing.

The blazetaur turned and bellowed at him, yanking its tail from the tree.

Erik didn't even flinch as he pulled out his sword. "I'm glad to see you saved it for me." He raised his sword above his head, a smile on his dirty face.

It was his fault we were even here hunting this thing, and I was more than glad to let him have the glory.

But Estrid wasn't. She and Erik were always competing. Sometimes it was cards. Sometimes women, and other times it was monsters. Who'd killed more blazetaurs? Who'd collected more shadebig body parts?

Maybe Erik was in the lead and that's what possessed Estrid to take a running leap onto the beast's swinging tail. She wasn't close enough to the stinger. She dug her sword into a meaty crevice, causing the monster to flick its tail. Hard.

Erik's eyes widened in surprise.

Estrid lost her grip and flew toward him.

He dropped his sword and made a valiant effort to catch her. They were almost the same size. Instead, she plowed into him like a boulder, sending both of them careening backward into a tree where they sat, stunned.

The blazetaur pawed the ground, raking a deep groove in the dirt.

Luckily, it seemed to have forgotten about me. Sometimes, as the youngest sister, it bothered me to be so forgettable that even the monsters on this blasted island ignored me. Other times, it was my greatest advantage. With my sword still in hand, I pulled my short-handled ax from my leather belt. I didn't fight with a shield. They weren't much use against monsters who could shatter them with one blow. But I was deadly with two blades.

As it drew its tail up to strike, I ran, taking long, quiet strides. My destination was a group of trees the monster had destroyed. The snapped trunks were positioned like a ramp. I hit them at full speed, slowing only slightly so as not to lose my balance. My eyes never left the tail. It was going to be close, but not impossible.

I didn't pause when I reached the top, where I was level with the monster's back. Instead, I leapt, feeling for a moment like a bird taking flight.

The tail passed just in front of me.

I hooked the blade of the ax around the stinger so I wouldn't fall, and stabbed my sword into its tail, meeting flesh.

And then I was falling. Just me and the stinger and a stream of warm, red blazetaur blood. The ground rushed to meet me. I hit it hard, all of the air rushing out of me at once.

The black stinger landed beside me, its point inches from my face. I gasped, unable to catch my breath.

The blazetaur swayed dangerously above me.

Hands were on me then, Erik's and Estrid's. They grabbed my vest, pulling me to my feet, pounding on my back as we ran for cover. The two of them dragged me as I regained my bearings.

We made it to the trees just as the monster collapsed with a crash that shook the ground. Its rear end hit first, the once-dangerous tail limp and lifeless. Then its front legs gave out. And finally its head, with its fang-like incisors, plowed into the dirt mere feet from our hiding place.

We all stared at the body in silence for a moment.

Erik turned narrowed eyes on me. "Do you ever think before you act?"

"If I did, you'd both be dead." I sheathed my sword and emerging back into the clearing. I kicked one of the blazetaur's gaping nostrils. Nothing. I moved past it, avoiding spikes and horns, until I saw what I was looking for. The stinger and, beneath it, the wooden handle of my ax. My name was carved into it in Ahvoli runes by my father before he'd given it to me on my thirteenth birthday.

Bracing a foot on the blazetaur's back for leverage, I tugged the ax free, careful not to touch the venom still leaking from the stinger.

Erik stood beside me, his eyes on my face. "I wish you wouldn't be so foolish sometimes. Your life is worth ten of mine." He clapped a hand on my shoulder. It was the closest to a "thank you" I would get from him.

"At least Luthair will be pleased." Estrid still had her swords drawn. It was wise to keep weapons readily at hand here, below the veil.

I grimaced involuntarily at the name of our benefactor, the governor. Barepost was the only human settlement on the island continent of Bruhier. Stephan Luthair controlled every-thing—the mine, the trade, the transportation. And us. The

Svand siblings owed him a debt, and Erik wouldn't let us leave until it was paid.

"Without honor, we are no better than the monsters that plague the island," Erik had said when I'd offered to sneak into Luthair's lavish home on the ridge and bury my ax in his gut, putting an end to our servitude once and for all. And so I never had, although I'd be lying if I said I wasn't tempted every time I looked up from our tiny rooms above the pub to see lights glowing in his luxurious glass windows. But I would do anything for Erik, even if it meant spending the last three years hunting brutish monsters and kowtowing to an obnoxious governor.

He had sent us after this blazetaur before it could reach the plateau where Barepost was situated. We'd spent the last twenty-four hours tracking it, doing our best to survive attacks from the myriad of monsters that lived below the veil.

The first hour had seen Erik nearly strangled by a trithon, a nasty, three-headed snake that lived in the trees and liked to drop down on top of its unsuspecting victims. Not long after that, we'd startled a fire elk and it caught Estrid's cloak on fire. Thankfully, she was unharmed, but her cloak lay in ashes somewhere on the forest floor. Part of our earnings from this job would have to go toward the purchase of a new one. Winters were unforgiving in Bruhier, and it looked like we would be here for another one.

I dropped the ax into my belt and turned to my brother. "Will he be happy?" I already knew the answer.

"Our job isn't over yet."

"It never is."

But Erik, used to my complaining, just smiled. "This was a female blazetaur."

Estrid and I raised our eyebrows at each other, not bothering to ask how he knew. Just as he was used to my complaining and Estrid's arguments, we were used to him knowing things.

"So now we have to find the nest." He stepped over the blazetaur's lolling black tongue and disappeared back into the tree line.

Estrid and I scurried behind him.

We walked for a long time, following a path of trampled trees. Thunder rumbled overhead. Though we couldn't see the veil of clouds from beneath the canopy of trees, I knew it would be grey and heavy with rain. I ran my hand along the trunk of a tree, tracing a deep groove that had almost certainly been made by a blazetaur horn. Estrid nodded at me approvingly. She was the best tracker of the three of us, but I wasn't bad and was getting better with her tutelage.

The ground leveled out as we walked. We were heading farther down the mountainside, deeper into monster territory. I followed Estrid and Erik and kept my eyes open for threats, because that was what I always did. I'd killed for them countless times, and I would die for them if I had to. As the littlest sister, I was no one without the two of them.

When the rain started, it drowned out all other sounds, making our trek downhill even more dangerous even though the water couldn't reach us through the canopy. We slipped our way down, one hill after another, until we finally emerged into a large clearing not unlike the one we had killed the blazetaur in. Fat drops of rain clung to my eyelashes, and I blinked them back, drawing my sword.

Erik placed his hand on my arm, telling me I didn't need it. He pointed. I followed the line of his finger to a group of massive boulders bunched together in the middle of the clearing.

Not boulders, I realized with a start.

Eggs.

Three of them leaning together in the middle of a ring of

toppled tree trunks. All of them taller than even Erik and wider than the three of us combined.

"The galestone won't ignite in the rain." Erik pulled the box of the volatile powder from inside his vest.

It was the only thing Luthair had given us before sending us down the mountain, one of his most valuable exports from the mine. He profited shamelessly from other countries at war, willing to send what they needed to destroy each other if the price was right.

Erik sat on a fallen log, returning the box and tinder to his vest for safekeeping while we waited for the rain to pass. I sat beside him while Estrid stood at the tree line, watching the nest as if she expected the eggs to hatch at any moment.

"I don't remember rain like this in the Western March." Here below the veil, it rained all the time, the forests steamy and muddy, the rivers constantly overflowing their banks.

"Maybe not," he said, "but do you remember the snow? It was even worse. It would freeze your eyes closed and turn your toes black."

"I miss the snow," I said wistfully.

That drew a chuckle from somewhere deep in his throat.

It wasn't the only thing I longed for. "I miss Dad."

"I miss his soup," Estrid chimed in.

Just the mention of the creamy dish loaded with lamb and pork and vegetables made my stomach grumble.

"Was that thunder?" Erik hit me in the shoulder lightly.

I hit him back, nearly sending him to the ground.

He caught himself and dusted off his hands. "I do forget you're not so little anymore."

"Just as you forget to feed me. You're a rotten big brother."

"We will eat." Erik said, "Just as soon as we are done."

The rain subsided soon after, leaving the ground in the clearing little more than churned mud. It sucked at our boots as we crossed to the nest and stood before the eggs. I rapped my knuckles on one shell, half-expecting to hear something stir inside in response. It remained still and quiet. My hand came away sticky with slime. I reached over and wiped it on Estrid's sleeve. She batted me away.

It did not escape my notice that there were three eggs, that there would be three siblings. Would one be the leader, the other two constantly nipping at his heels? Would the youngest be reckless and impulsive, with the oldest constantly pulling her back from the edge while the middle sibling rolled her eyes and tried to reason with them both? There was a pang in my chest, but it was something I was used to ignoring.

"Do not feel bad." Erik seemed to be reading my thoughts. "The hatchlings would fight to the death as soon as they emerged. Only one of them would have survived anyway." He carefully pulled back the lid on the box of galestone.

"And we would have been sent to hunt it before too long. Why don't you let me light it?" Estrid held a hand out for the flint.

Erik shooed us both away. "You and Frida take cover."

We didn't have any direct experience with galestone, but not long after we'd arrived in Barepost, there'd been an explosion in the mine. It had blown a hole in the mountainside.

For once, neither of us argued.

I followed Estrid into the forest at a fast clip, moving back up the mountain until we came to a rocky overhang.

"Here." She pulled me down beside her so our backs were against the warm rock, situated between us and the clearing.

My legs burned with the effort of running uphill, but my breaths were steady and quiet as I listened for Erik.

"Should we go back for him?" I knew better, but I couldn't help asking.

Estrid shook her head. "No. He'll make it. He always does."

I imagined him setting the charge, unrolling the line and sprinkling it with galestone. Striking the flint and dropping it, watching to make sure it caught, which would steal valuable time from his escape.

"He should be here."

"He's coming."

Just then, he launched himself over the rock and pressed his body against ours. Taking his cue, Estrid and I ducked low and covered our ears, a ball of Svands.

The explosion rocked the ground and rang in my ears. Even this far away, dirt and debris flew over our hiding place. A jagged piece of grey, slimy shell hit the ground just in front of us, sticking into it like a blade.

Erik peeled himself away from us, his dirty face blank with shock.

"Well," I said when the ringing had subsided. "Can we eat now?"

Our laughter followed us back up the hill to Barepost where a warm meal, a semi-comfortable bed, and a sleazy governor waited for our return.

CHAPTER 2

Unfortunately, the sleazy governor was the first to greet us when we ambled through the town's gate. We were dirty and tired and nearly delirious with hunger.

He stood at the gate, and as the guards on duty raised the portcullis that separated Barepost from the dangers of life below the veil, it revealed him inch by inch until we were finally face to face with him.

He narrowed his coal-black eyes at us. "You couldn't have been more subtle? The blast nearly caused a cave-in." He shook invisible dust off the front of his robes. In a town coated in ash and dust, he was the cleanest person I'd ever seen.

"Oh." Estrid held a hand held to her heart. "Did we not blow up a vicious, man-eating monster quietly enough for you? How much of our pay will you dock us this time?"

She was crabby but rightfully so. We'd hardly eaten or slept in over a day and had just finished scaling the side of a mountain—the last several hundred feet a nearly vertical climb—just to reach the town. It was located on a slight rise about midway up the side of the plateau's cliff face.

"You'll be lucky if you get any pay at all."

All of us—even magnanimous Erik—ignored him as we followed the dirt road.

Luthair followed, complaining.

As we rounded a small bend, Barepost unfolded before us in all of its miserable glory. We were still below the veil, so neither the sun nor the moons shone through significantly. The plateau itself was below the veil, as well, which was odd for this area. Almost all of the plateaus were above the layer of clouds that seemed to always be there.

Barepost was a colorless town of dust with dirt roads and flat, brown storefronts that gave way to flat, brown houses with crumbling yards that turned to pools of mud when it rained. Which was often. The streets were always half-empty at this hour. Most people were too exhausted to do anything but go home and go to bed at the end of a long day in the mines.

Our destination was the pub, an old, ramshackle three-story building that was easily the nicest one in town. A wooden sign above the door swung on squeaky hinges. The Gold Mine Inn & Pub. The name seemed entirely too optimistic to me. No one had ever extracted gold from these mines.

Gerves, the owner, said it was ironic, but I wasn't fooled. He also said that opening the Gold Mine had been his lifelong dream. Another lie. No one came to Barepost with a dream to settle here. It was a place where people got stuck on their way to somewhere better. A place where living meant surviving. Not thriving, and certainly not dreaming.

We banged through the door into the dark room, drawing all eyes to us as usual. Most everyone in Barepost was human. With our half-elven heritage, we couldn't go anywhere without being noticed, which was how most people in Barepost came to know us, though not many liked us. But I didn't care. With the exception of a select few, I didn't like them either.

Every time we walked in here, I was reminded of the first

time, when Estrid and I had come in battered and bruised and begged Gerves for a room. It hadn't been our finest moment, but to be fair, Erik had been on his deathbed. After crashing on Bruhier, we'd dragged his unconscious body up the mountain, fighting off monsters and torrential downpours, until finally taking refuge in Barepost. Luthair—with his connections and his money—had saved him when neither of us could. But when it came to Luthair, nothing was free, and we were still here three years later, working off that life-debt.

He followed us in as we wove through the tables and squeezed into a booth in the back. He slid in beside me.

I glared at Estrid.

She smirked and shrugged as if to say, "Better you than me."

The booth suddenly felt ten times too small. If I could, I would have crawled out from beneath the table and ran for it, but there was no way I would fit.

"You need to get your women under control." Luthair's leg pressed against mine as he leaned forward and glared at Erik. "I'm the only one who can afford your exorbitant rates and the only one who can forgive you of your debt. You should all show me a little more respect."

"If you don't like it, perhaps it's time for us to move on." I rubbed a hand down my tired face and scanned the room for Grissall, the serving girl and Gerves's daughter.

He turned to me, his breath on my cheek.

I cringed and leaned away.

"Respect."

"Respect is earned," Estrid said coolly.

"You think I haven't earned respect? Who saved your brother's life? Who keeps Barepost running? Who keeps it from turning into a lawless free-for-all?" He slapped his hands on the table so loudly that other patrons near to us turned.

When they saw Luthair, though, they spun away.

"Me. That's who."

Estrid opened her mouth again.

But we were saved by Grissall, Gerves's daughter and serving girl. She set down four mugs of lukewarm ale and stepped back. She smoothed her dull brown smock and glanced nervously at the governor. "You want some stew? I think there's enough left."

"Yes, please," Erik said, answering for all of us.

Grissall disappeared into the crowd.

"Back to the matter at hand." Luthair straightened, his chin forward.

"Our payment?" Estrid interrupted.

"Our freedom?" I added.

"Your incompetence." Luthair looked dryly at Erik.

Erik put a hand on Estrid's arm just as she was drawing a breath. Then he lifted his ale, took two large swallows, and banged it back on the table. His thick, golden beard had traces of foam in it. "We did the job you gave us with the tools you provided. We had an agreement, and I have honored my part. I don't know what is up for discussion."

Luthair glowered at Erik and Estrid in turn, then lowered his gaze on me.

As uncomfortable as I was, I refused to squirm.

He reached into his pocket and pulled out a leather purse cinched with twine, and dropped it heavily on the table. The coins inside clinked together.

It took every ounce of self-restraint I had not to reach over and snatch it away.

Erik drained his mug and then slid the purse toward him as casually as if we didn't need the money, as if our very existence didn't depend on it. "I assume you've kept your portion?"

"Yes. One-quarter, as agreed."

I didn't know how much we'd paid or how much was still due. I didn't know what value they'd put on my brother's life, but I didn't ask. Neither of them would ever tell me, anyway. I would stay here as long as Erik needed me to.

Grissall returned, four bowls balanced on her scrawny arms. "Here we are, then." She deftly set a bowl before each of us.

I thought Luthair might gag looking down into the lumpy broth. "What is this?"

"Pa's stew. He makes it every week from whatever is left over. Everyone loves it."

Well, that was a gross exaggeration, but to emphasize her point, I scooped a giant spoonful into my mouth. "Delicious," I said around a mouthful of meat from an undetermined source.

Grissall grinned, the smile changing her face. It made her look her actual age instead of like an old woman. "I'll give Pa your compliments."

"Better to give him this," Erik said, flipping two coins from the pouch to pay for this week's and next week's room and board. Gerves was one of the only men in town who didn't hate us, so Erik hated being late on any payment to him. I thought there was a part of him who felt indebted to the innkeeper more than we already were. He had, after all, taken pity on Estrid and me when we'd come crawling to him for refuge.

"Better to return my plate to the kitchen." Luthair pushed the bowl away.

I dragged the governor's bowl in front of me. "No need to waste it. Make sure you pay the girl before you go."

Luthair's face turned a lovely shade of tomato red. If he'd been a dragon, I thought it likely smoke would be pouring from his ears, not that I'd ever seen a dragon.

He dropped two coins on the table and gathered his robes around him. "Stay close." He ignored Estrid and I like we didn't exist. "You never know when I may call on you again."

We finished the rest of our meal in a comfortable silence.

I watched without saying anything as Erik tossed back mug after mug of the sour ale long after Estrid and I had switched to water. It brought the color back to his cheeks and loosened his tense muscles, and neither of us could begrudge him that release.

When I'd finished off two bowls of the bland stew, more out of duty than desire, Erik and Estrid took seats at the card table with a group of locals. They'd gotten used to us through the years and had no problem taking a bit of our coin.

With a full belly, my eyes were drooping. So I decided to head upstairs to the room I shared with Estrid. No one else saw me go, but I waved goodnight to Gerves, who stood behind his polished bar, drying a mug and keeping an eye on the card game. He raised his chin in acknowledgment.

Up the creaking wooden stairs, our room was last on the left, just past Erik's room and joined to his by an inner door. The room was dark but familiar enough that I didn't have to waste wax by burning a candle. Only Luthair, in his fancy house on the ridge, had gas lamps. We had one trunk that held all our meager belongings. I sat on it to remove my boots and my filthy clothes. Then I crossed to the wash basin on the dresser and did my best to clean myself without being able to take an actual bath. The water was chilly and raised goosebumps on my bare arms.

When I was done, I donned my spare pants and tunic and stood at the window, pulling back the heavy curtain to get a good view of the sky.

Both moons were visible from here—Aupra, pale and low on the horizon, and Gleet, the watcher who never slept, his blue expanse a constant presence in the sky no matter where we were.

It was strange to me that these were the same moons I'd watched with my father from our home in Bor'sur. The harbor town where I'd grown up was the largest in the Western March, situated on a massive outcropping of rock a thousand feet above the water.

"This is the closest to Gleet you'll ever get, my star," my father would say, holding me up above his head so I could try to reach for him. "Remember that when you are traveling the world. That you'll always have to come back to visit him."

It occurred to me only later, after I'd already left, that my father was my moon.

And I was his star.

I lifted a hand to my face and traced the mark beside my eye, the brown, five-pointed stain that appeared only after my mother had left. She'd been my father's second wife, marrying him after Erik and Estrid's mother had died giving birth to Estrid. She'd arrived in Bor'sur alone, a stranger in a dangerous place, and my father had taken her in. To hear my father speak of it, she was there one day and gone the next, as quietly as if she had never been there at all. He hadn't remarried again but had raised the three of us on his own.

Estrid and Erik, both still very young when she left, had little memory of her, though still more than I did. Erik said she was soft-spoken but firm, a warrior with words, not swords. Estrid didn't speak of her. Erik said it was because she'd lost two mothers and blamed herself, just as she blamed herself for sending us on the errand that brought us to Bruhier.

I lifted the wooden window frame a crack. A sliver of cool air slipped inside and brushed my damp skin. I crawled beneath the scratchy blanket—a far cry from the luxurious furs I remembered from home in Bor'sur—and let sleep take me.

CHAPTER 3

The next morning, I didn't rise until noon. Estrid was still snoring indelicately on her side of the bed, the blanket thrown over her face to block out the sun coming through the open window. I gathered our travel-worn clothes we'd discarded the night before and went downstairs, where I gave them to Grissall to launder.

At the bar, Gerves slid a bowl of porridge in front of me without a word. I dug in. The two of us were the only ones in the pub, and we sat in amiable silence while I ate.

When I finished, he leaned his elbows on the bar and studied me. "The *Green Gem* came in last night."

My heart stuttered but I kept my face impassive. The *Gem* was one of Luthair's trading ships. It left loaded with stones, gems, and minerals, and returned months later with bags of fresh food, fine fabrics, and exotic spices.

Harbin, my only actual friend in Barepost, worked on-board, and he always brought me news of the world beyond Bruhier—wars and assassinations and royal weddings. And he always kept an ear to the ground for anything about the D'ahvol or the Western March. Luthair had never fostered a relationship with my people, but other traders had, and I was desperate for any news from home, even if it was just to know that the place still existed. That was easy to forget at times, isolated as we were on this blasted island.

But I also worried for Harbin. The trade passage was dangerous, and we had grown close in spite of my determination to keep my distance. "What news?" I didn't want to admit I was nervous to hear his answer. If I lost Harbin, I'd lose my only connection to the outside world and my only friend.

"They say it was an easy passage."

Some tight knot inside of me loosened a little. I stood maybe too eagerly. The barstool screeched loudly against the stone floor. "I think I'll just go." I pointed to the door. "If Erik or Estrid ask for me—"

"I'll tell them you're at the wharf," Gerves said with a smile.

Outside was a bustle of eager activity as the shop owners prepared to receive the *Gem's* delivery, and the residents prepared to spend what little money they had on luxuries they didn't need.

Aysche, Luthair's niece, hustled by with a gaggle of her friends. She wore a heavy velvet dress inlaid with gold and, like her uncle, seemed somehow immune to the dust that settled over everyone else.

"Oh, look," she said in her whiny voice, her eyes finding me in the street. "I didn't think we allowed monsters inside the gates. I must remember to urge my uncle to strengthen the guards."

I ignored her, breezing past. Her words used to bother me, but that was before I saw her for what she was. She was always as shiny as a new coin, but beneath the shine, she was uglier than anyone here.

"Is she mute?" asked one of her friends.

"No, just daft, like all of the D'ahvol. Stupid, brutish mutts."

Aysche's cruel words froze me in my tracks. All thoughts of

ignoring her were pushed out by the rage that boiled up inside of me. I whirled on her, stopping the group of girls in their tracks. I was at least a foot taller than her, if not more.

Her eyes went from my broad chest to my hand on the head of my ax before she steeled herself and met my gaze.

"What did you say?" I asked in a cold, quiet voice. It felt like we were in a bubble.

The crowd parted around us and grew quiet.

Aysche smirked, but her eyes darted sideways as if looking for help. "You heard me."

That I did. "I was giving you a chance to take it back."

"I won't." She drew herself up to her full height even while the girls around her shrank back. "It's the truth."

It would be so easy to prove her right, to pull the ax and cut her down, to be a brute and a monster. What was stopping me? The thought of punishment by Luthair? I could end him just as easily, tear a path through Barepost.

But what about Erik and Estrid? I tried to picture the disappointment on Erik's face, tried to make myself care even though I longed to soak Aysche's pretty dress in her own blood.

"Frida!" a male voice broke through my anger, and the bubble that had been building inside of me deflated.

Harbin cut through the crowd. He was my age, and close to my size even though he swore he didn't have any D'ahvol blood in him. But where I was light, he was dark, with skin that didn't burn in the sun and thick black hair that he kept cropped close to his head. In his months at sea, his beard had grown in, covering half of his handsome face. He wore lightweight linen pants and a matching tunic belted with a leather vest, his short-bladed sword swinging lazily at his side.

"Look who the tide dragged in." I turned away from Aysche.

"Just the D'ahvol I was looking for." Harbin pulled me into a hug. He smelled like the sea, salty and fresh and maybe a little fishy.

So I did, refusing to give Luthair's niece any more of my attention. But it wasn't completely unselfish. I knew ignoring her, more than anything, would anger her.

Harbin kept one arm around my shoulder, steering me away.

Aysche said nothing more.

Once we'd cleared the crowd by the shops and turned onto the small road leading to the wharf, Harbin turned to me. "Can't keep out of trouble, can you?" He waved at an older sailor passing the other way with a keg thrown over his shoulders. The man nodded first at Harbin, then at me.

"What fun would that be?" I relaxed the farther we got from Aysche.

As we walked, he told me where they'd gone on this trip. They'd followed the great river Gathredelle from the shining cities of Abrecem Secer to the tree groves of the Southern Plains. He'd seen elves and dragons, trolls and merfolk, things I'd only ever heard of before.

I listened intently, trying to imagine it all. It was the life I had imagined for myself with Estrid and Erik, traveling to distant lands, finding adventure and fame and riches. It was hard to believe, sometimes, that all that beauty was out there while I was stuck here with monsters straight out of a child's nightmares.

"Why do you keep coming back to Barepost?" I asked. The sun peeked briefly through the veil, and I raised my face to it.

"It's home," he said with a shrug. "It calls me back."

I knew what he meant.

We finally reached the dock. The ocean stretched out as far as I could see, curving along the horizon, glowing yellow and green and blue in the light of the afternoon sun. The *Green Gem* was docked at the wharf, the largest ship in the port. Its two masts reached high, its vibrant green sails furled around the booms.

Men and women traipsed back and forth with bags and

boxes and kegs, dropping them on the wooden pier where others waited to load them onto the lifts. Not far from us, the lift operators heaved the ropes against the pulleys, bringing the goods up to the cliff face, where still more people waited to receive them and deliver them into Barepost proper.

"Want to go down?" Harbin asked after a load had been raised.

I loved visiting the wharf, loved how busy it was and how free it felt.

We stepped onto the platform, the only two passengers going back down. Holding on to one of the ropes, I leaned far out over the edge to watch our descent and the activity below us.

"Steady, now, gentlemen," Harbin said.

The lift operators obliged, letting us down to the beach slow and steady. Harbin's hand found mine and held on tight. He wasn't such a fan of heights. Thankfully, we made it down without incident.

On the wooden dock, Harbin stopped walking and put a hand on my shoulder. "There's something I haven't told you."

"What?" I turned to him, scanning his face.

"I brought you something."

"Something?"

"Well, someone, really."

My first thought was that it was my father. I turned back to the boat, my eyes searching the throngs of people for a familiar face. Would he have changed much in these last few years? Would his hair have gone grey? Were the smile lines around his eyes and mouth deeper? Did he even smile anymore, with all of his children lost and his wives dead or gone?

But I didn't see him. I didn't see anyone except for the familiar faces of the residents and merchants and sailors of Barepost, people who were becoming commonplace to me.

"Frida." Harbin put a hand on my elbow and drew me

forward just as two women approached us. "This is Tsarra Trisfina, high elf of Lamruil, and her companion, Savarah. Tsarra, this is Frida, youngest of the Svand siblings."

"Hello," I said, looking sideways at Harbin. I'd been hoping for a gift, and this . . . well, this was disappointing. I had no idea why he was introducing me to these strange women or why they'd brought a high elf into Barepost at all. If I thought I got strange looks, this Trisfina lady would have it a hundred times worse. The two of us together—well, we ought to charge people to stare.

"Frida." Tsarra gently grasped one of my hands in both of hers. She was tall and slender and elegant, everything I always thought an elf might be. I couldn't really tell if she was beautiful. Her features were sharp with a wide, flat brow. Her long, pointed ears were decorated with jewelry. She wore a white dress and a grey feathered cloak fastened with a golden strap across her chest. "I cannot tell you how pleased I am to finally meet you."

"You are?" I still had no idea what was going on. Harbin was no help. He stood to the side, rocking back on his heels and looking very pleased with himself.

"Oh, yes," said Savarah, taking my hand from her friend. She was conventionally beautiful with golden curls and a wide, rosy face. She was also human.

In spite of that, when she touched me, a rush of something like anger made my head spin. I extracted my hand as delicately as possible. I had no idea what that was, but I didn't want her to touch me again.

"Master Harbin told us all about you and your siblings." Savarah didn't seem bothered by or even seem to notice my unease as she sidled closer to me. "I convinced Tsarra that you would be her best hope."

"You're getting ahead of yourself." Tsarra scolded her friend. Then to me, "Perhaps there's somewhere we can talk in private?

I would like to discuss a job of the utmost importance and discretion."

A job? From someone other than Luthair? It seemed too good to be true. I pulled Harbin aside. "Where did they come from?"

"We stopped at Lamruil a few days ago." He glanced over my shoulder apologetically.

I jerked on his sleeve to bring his attention back to me.

He brought his face close to mine and dropped his voice to a whisper. "They paid a lot for passage to Barepost. They're looking for someone in the mines from what I gather. I might have mentioned that you, Erik, and Estrid would be willing to help for the right price."

"And what is the price?"

"I don't think it matters. Name it and they'll pay it. I thought this could be it for you, you know? Make enough money to buy your way home. No more sneaking onto ships at midnight or hunting down monsters for a pittance."

I looked back at the women, turning his words over in my head. Elves didn't typically deal with anyone outside of their race, but here was this high-born Bruish elf with a human companion asking a D'ahvol for help. If she could travel all this way and take a chance on me, maybe we could take a chance on her.

"Fine. Follow me."

CHAPTER 4

When our strange parade—minus Harbin who had to stay and work—burst into the Gold Mine, I thought Gerves's eyes were going to pop out of their sockets. Luckily, the only other customers were my siblings. They sat at our usual table, bowls of what looked to be leftover stew in front of them.

Estrid stood, her hand on the swords at her hips.

Erik grew very still, his eyes finding first Tsarra, then Savarah, and then me. "What's this?"

I procured two chairs. "Two mugs of your finest ale," I called to Gerves.

He rolled his eyes. There was only one ale in Barepost, and it was good enough for everyone. Still, he reached up to pull down two mugs from the rack and turned his back on us to fill them from the keg.

Savarah sat without hesitation.

Tsarra was slower to acclimate to her surroundings, looking around with distaste at the dark innards of the pub. I imagined that pubs in Lamruil were much classier, with crystal serving platters and wide windows to brighten the walls. Here, glass was far too expensive, and windows let in the dust just as easily as the sun and weren't worth the hassle. Unless you were Stephan Luthair, who could pay people to keep his windows clean and sweep his floors.

Erik noticed Tsarra's scowl and turned his hooded eyes on me as if he could extract an explanation from my face.

All I gave him, though, was a wan smile and a nod of my head.

Once we'd all sat, our party of five squeezed in tightly around the square table, and Gerves had brought everyone their ale, we stared at one another for a brief moment.

Estrid turned to me, wasting no time on pleasantries or introductions. "Why have you brought them here? Who are they?"

"That question is, perhaps, best directed to Mistress Trisfina?" Savarah gestured with her hand.

Estrid shifted her gaze to Tsarra. "Fine. Who are you, and why are you here?"

"My name is Tsarra Trisfina," the elf woman answered, her voice gentle like the ringing of small bells. "I am searching for a high-born elf of Lamruil, a man called Arun Phina."

"There are no elves here." Estrid waved a hand in dismissal.

"There should not be, no." Tsarra shook her head. "But I have it on good faith that Governor Luthair took Arun in an unlawful bargain and enslaved him in the mines."

"What sort of unlawful bargain?" Erik still hadn't dropped his guard in spite of his outward appearance of calm.

I knew that any minute, he could stand and order the women away and this chance at freedom would be squandered just as all the others had been before.

"A life bargain," Tsarra answered. "He traded one of his imprisoned miners for Arun Phina."

"Why would your Arun Phina make such a bargain?" Erik's voice was tense as he waited for an answer. He was stuck in his own type of life bargain, one that Estrid and I had made for him.

Tsarra didn't seem entirely sure how to answer. She leaned her head from one side to the other, thinking. "Our Arun will die for a cause he believes in. The creature your governor—"

"Not," I interrupted, "our governor."

"The creature Governor Luthair," Tsarra corrected herself, "had imprisoned was innocent of his crimes, and when Arun found out, it became his mission to free him. No matter the cost. Even if the cost meant his life."

"So he's imprisoned in the mines, and you want us to?" Estrid raised her eyebrows expectantly.

"Free him. Break into the mine and free him."

Erik barked a laugh as he shifted in his chair. Without another sound, he lifted his mug and drained it, a drop of brown liquid dampening his beard.

"Are you not the best?" Savarah smiled across the table at Erik, but it wasn't a kind look.

"The best what, exactly?" Estrid leaned forward, her guard up.

Savarah's gaze slid to her over her untouched mug of ale. "We've heard about the three of you even in Lamruil. The Svand siblings for hire. You kill the monsters and protect the people, don't you? How is what we're asking any different?"

"What we're good at is surviving." Estrid's cheeks flushed. She was normally even-keeled, but something about Savarah seemed to get a rise out of her. I put a hand on her arm, but she didn't seem to notice. "We don't do the things we do to protect the *people*. We do what we do to protect *ourselves*."

"But," I jumped in before the situation could deteriorate even further. "For the right price . . ." I trailed off, hoping Tsarra would fill in the blanks. This was going badly. All we needed was one chance. Was that too much to ask?

But Tsarra kept her eyes on her own mug, spinning it in lazy circles between her fingers.

"The price doesn't matter." Erik might as well have closed a book with that sentence. "The cost is too high."

"The cost?" Tsarra looked up.

"We would go to war with Luthair, and Luthair doesn't play fair. We would be making our own life bargains. Ours for your Arun Phina's."

"Not if Tsarra is able to guarantee us immediate passage out of Barepost." I didn't even know if that was the case, but I had to throw it out there.

"The only thing I can guarantee," Tsarra said, "is that the high elves will go to war with Barepost to get Arun back. That seems like a high price to pay for your refusal to help."

"It appears you're in a bit of a rough situation." Savarah kept her smile in place and shook her head.

"I am sorry for your Arun Phina," Erik said, pushing himself to his feet. "But he entered into this bargain on his own. We will not be able to help you."

"Erik—" I started. This couldn't be the end.

"My answer is no."

I snapped my mouth shut, embarrassed by his easy dismissal. I was tired of being ignored and closed out, when all I wanted was to save us. "And why should we listen to you?"

Erik dropped back down into his seat and watched me, an astonished expression on his face. "Because you always do."

He was right. We did. So why was I fighting this so hard? It was like I had two voices inside of my head—my usual, fairly reasonable one and another one, unfamiliar in its anger and righteousness. I had a temper, yes, but it wasn't typically directed at my brother.

Estrid glanced from me to Erik, and then to Savarah, who watched our exchange with barely-concealed excitement.

Tsarra, on the other hand, squirmed uncomfortably in her

seat, looking anywhere but at the three of us. "We should go. It's clear our trip here was in vain."

"Quite so," Savarah agreed, not taking her eyes off Erik. She dropped two coins onto the table as she stood. "For our drinks." Then they breezed out the door.

As soon as they were gone, the tension disappeared, like a knot being unwound. Erik's shoulders slumped forward. Estrid fell backward into her chair.

But I was still furious. "Why would you turn them down? You barely even gave them a chance."

"Frida, I—"

"All Luthair has to do is say jump, and you ask how high, but I bring us something else—a real, valid option—and you don't even consider it." I was yelling.

Gerves pushed Grissall toward the back, the movement small but the message clear. This sort of dispute was dangerous and unwelcome here.

"That's not fair," Estrid said. "You don't know—"

I couldn't take it anymore, couldn't sit here and listen to them justify our situation. I stood, my own restless energy finally getting the better of me. "I know I hate this place. I know I hate Stephan Luthair, and I know he likely owes this elf his freedom. And I know I cannot spend the rest of my life here beneath his thumb."

I barreled out the door without giving them a chance to do anything to stop me.

The street was still busy, packed with people carrying brown paper packages and shouting back and forth to one another. A group of sailors was heading to the Gold Mine so I turned away from them and walked in the opposite direction. It was then that I saw a slip of white dress disappear around the corner of the general store.

On a whim, I followed, stopping at the mouth to the alleyway, listening.

"All is not lost," Savarah was saying. "We will find a way."

"Without him," Tsarra said, her voice thick with tears. She sniffed and continued, "Without our marriage . . . Oh, I cannot bear the thought of never returning home again. Of my parents and sisters being cast out of Lamruil. Where will we go? How will we survive?"

Interesting. So it seemed the mission was more personal than political. There would be no army coming down from Lamruil to attack Barepost and free the high-born elf imprisoned in the mines. It wasn't even love for Arun Phina that had driven Tsarra down from her high rock. It was love for her family, a desire and a responsibility to keep them safe.

I came around the corner finally. Tsarra looked up at me from where she leaned against the wall of the general store, her arms crossed over her stomach as if in pain. Savarah took a step away from her, turning toward me in surprise.

"I'll do it," I said, "but not for free."

"I cannot pay you." Tsarra stepped away from the wall.

I held up a hand to stop her. "I don't want your coins. If I do this thing, Luthair will punish me, and if he cannot punish me, then he will punish my brother and sister. No amount of money will buy our safety on Barepost. We will need to leave with you and Arun Phina, and I want you to promise us shelter in Lamruil and passage back to the Western March."

"I don't—"

"Done," Savarah said, interrupting Tsarra's objections.

"Savarah!" Tsarra whipped her head toward her friend, her voice sharper than I'd yet heard from her. "I'm in no position to make any such promises."

"Perhaps not," Savarah said unabashedly, looking wholly unconcerned. "But Arun Phina will be if she gets him out. And if she doesn't—" She shrugged. "Well, we won't owe her a thing."

I took a few steps into the alley and reached a hand out to Tsarra.

The elf looked at it, then up at me, and finally took my hand, sealing our deal. As soon as her skin touched mine, I felt a rush of excitement I hadn't felt in a long time, not even when I'd sliced off the blazetaur's poisonous stinger. I would finally be going up against the real monster in Barepost—Governor Stephan Luthair. And I definitely didn't like to lose.

CHAPTER 5

There was a single entrance to Barepost's mine. It sat high above Barepost itself, carved into the side of the mountain. It was there that I found myself the next morning, watching the day's miners plod carefully to work. The pathway up was treacherous, rocky and barely wide enough for one man. They walked single file, a rope tied to a beam at the top linking them together. There were lifts like at the wharf, but here, they were reserved for raising and lowering goods, not men. I knew that the mine housed prisoners who lived, worked, ate, and slept below ground, but a lot of men from Barepost worked there too. They were the ones who came and went every day, risking the trip to go home to their families at night.

This was the only entrance and exit. It wasn't just a matter of finding a way in, but of sneaking back out with a prisoner. There had to be another way.

"There's no other way."

I jerked, toppling over in my hiding place, sending a cloud of dust into the air. I coughed and waved my hand in front of my face, then looked up to see Erik standing over me. He squatted down beside me, his form barely hidden by the thin vegetation growing wild on the hill, and squinted over at the procession creeping up the mountain.

"What?"

"I know what you're thinking, and there's no other way in or out of the mine."

We hadn't talked since I'd stormed out of the pub the day before. It was the longest we'd gone without talking, at least while both of us were conscious.

"And you'll never get in undetected."

I whipped my head around toward this new voice.

Estrid was on my other side, ducking low into the grass. The three of us blended into the landscape with our brown leather armor and fur cloaks and hair the color of straw. We were far enough away that if one of the workers were to look over this way, they'd see nothing out of place.

"It's part of why I couldn't take this job," Erik said. "But I assume you did?"

"I did." I tried to sound confident. "Someone has to get us off this island."

"This isn't the way."

"Arun Phina will give us transport to Lamruil, and then Tsarra Trisfina will guarantee us safe passage back to the Western March."

"You made a deal with an absent man?" Estrid scoffed. "You'd risk our lives on the off chance that this elf will feel some sort of gratitude when we free him from a situation he willingly walked into? Have you ever known a Bruish elf to worry about anyone other than themselves?"

"Tsarra said he is a man of his word and with the means to back it up."

"Tsarra Trisfina will say anything to get her way." Estrid sneered at me. It was a look she typically reserved for outsiders. For people she deemed daft or unworthy. The fact that it was aimed at me made something inside of me shrink.

I'd felt it at times through the years, the differences between us. We all got our looks from our father, so that made it easier to fit in with them, but there was always a bond between them that I never did quite share. It showed up in small moments throughout our childhood, when they would gang up on me or stand side by side and squeeze me out without even thinking about it. I'd spent my whole life scrambling to keep up and to fit in, and I was tired of it. I was going to do this job and prove them wrong. I was a Svand, just like the two of them.

I turned to Erik, ignoring my sister. "You've been in there, right?" Luthair had sent Erik and a small squadron into the mines to extract a gloomling.

"All the more reason not to return."

"You must know your way around, though. If I can get in, can you tell me where to find the prisoners?"

"Whether or not I can doesn't matter." Erik shook his head, his eyes on the mine entrance. "You're not going in."

"I am." The mine workers disappeared into the dark tunnel, and the distant sound of echoing hammers and squeaking carts rang from the entrance. "With or without your help."

They both stood as if connected by a string I couldn't see.

"Without, then," Estrid said. "Good luck."

"It's not about luck," I shouted at their retreating backs, all semblance of stealth gone. "It's cunning and planning and bravery."

"You have the last in spades," Estrid said over her shoulder. "Maybe someday you'll admit that you need us for the other two."

As I stood there and watched their retreating backs, I realized she was probably right. But I would never admit it, not in a million years.

I stayed on the hill until nightfall. I spent my time wallowing in self-pity. I'd never felt so alone. Not just physically alone but alone in my decisions. I'd always shared my steps with Erik and

Estrid, and been glad to do so, but I couldn't help but feel they were leading me down the wrong path this time, blindfolds over their eyes.

When no one had come to get me by the time even the miners had gone home, I decided it was time to swallow a bit of my pride and return to the pub. My stomach growled, desperate for something to fill it, even if it was Gerves's stew. The walk back to town was uneventful, though I kept expecting Aysche to lunge at me out of the shadows just to really round out a truly awful day.

She didn't. The streets were practically empty, everyone at home enjoying dinner. I thought about going to the rooming house where Harbin stayed instead and trying to bum dinner off of his landlord, but decided against it. The old lady who ran the rooming house was grumpy on a good day and was just as likely to run me off as to pull out a chair for me. The pub was at least a sure thing.

I was both disappointed and relieved that when I arrived. The pub was crawling with patrons, but none of them were related to me. I stood in the doorway, surveying the crowd.

Grissall rushed past me, not even glancing in my direction, a pitcher of water in one hand and a tray of loaded plates in the other. There was a group of miners in one corner, given away by the grime on their faces and clothes and the way their shoulders slumped with exhaustion over their mugs of ale. Some sailors were here, too, but Harbin was nowhere to be seen.

But what drew my attention the most was the figure at the bar.

A woman wearing a deep-purple dress, her thick golden hair falling in loose waves down her back. It was Savarah, leaning on the bar. When she saw me watching, she raised a glass at me with a small twist of her lips.

I cut through the crowd and approached her, dropping back the hood of my cloak.

"Drink?" Gerves asked me from behind the bar.

"No, thanks." I turned to Savarah. "Where is Tsarra?"

"Gone," Savarah answered shortly.

"Gone?"

"Back to Lamruil on a ship that departed at midday."

"What about Arun Phina?"

She waved a hand up and down the length of her body. "That's why I'm here. Her trusted advisor to oversee the rescue mission." She took another long drink from her mug and then set it back on the counter, turning away and looking over the dining room. "It's strange . . ."

"What?" I surveyed the room with her. It looked pretty normal to me, though there was a subtle tension passing over the gathered diners, a whisper starting at one end of the room and rolling from ear to ear.

"This place hasn't changed a bit, not in all these years."

"This place? You mean you've been here before?" I laughed mirthlessly. "Why would you come back?"

One of the sailors glanced over his shoulder at one of the miners, then whispered to a friend. Grissall walked between them, glancing nervously around. She felt it too.

"Barepost born and raised," Savarah said. "My father worked in these very mines. But it was a long time ago."

I looked at her sideways, eyes skimming over her smooth skin. "It couldn't have been that long ago."

This time, she laughed. "Longer than you might think."

"How did you leave?" I asked her. "It doesn't seem that many people do."

Her eyes grew distant, and even though she was watching the dining room, I knew she wasn't seeing it. "It's crazy, the things a girl will do for love."

The room erupted. Even though I'd had my eyes on the diners, I didn't see how it happened. All of a sudden, men were leaping back from tables, scattering dishes and chairs, and two of them were lunging at each other. I pushed off of the bar.

Savarah didn't move, her eyes on the brawl as if it were a beautiful work of art meant to be admired.

"We have to stop them!" I shouted at her.

She waved a slender hand at me in obvious dismissal. "Why put an end to all the fun?" Her eyes sparkled.

Gerves came around the bar, a galestone pistol in one hand. It was a rare and dangerous weapon, and firing it in this crowd would only create more chaos. I followed him, leaving Savarah behind.

"You get the miner," I told him and then launched myself at the sailor who straddled the other man, pummeling him in the face and chest. He and I rolled, his fists still swinging.

"Someone has gone for the guard," Grissall's raspy voice shouted over the din.

"Let them come." The miner strained against Gerves's hold on his arms.

I was glad to at least see him on his feet, but the distraction got the better of me when the sailor's fist connected with my jaw. I slammed the unfamiliar man's head back against the stone floor with just enough force to stun him. When he looked up at me, he blinked once, then again, like a man just waking up, confused by his surroundings.

Before I could ask him any questions, though, the door burst open, and three men in uniform thundered inside, louder than anything else in the room.

I jerked the sailor to his feet. He was still moving slow, holding one hand to his head.

"I already looked," I told him. "You're not bleeding."

The guard, a younger man I'd often seen trailing Luthair, bound the sailor's hands with a length of rope and grabbed him by his collar. "Let's go. A couple days down below ought to be enough to cool you off. Then maybe you'll think twice about throwing punches in any of our fine establishments."

That was it.

As I watched them go and the others began to put the room back to rights, the spark of an idea, which had been a mere ember in the dark, caught fire and roared to life.

"Are you all right, Frida?" Savarah asked, a hand on my shoulder.

A shiver snaked its way from my shoulder down my spine. I turned away from her, hoping not to make it too obvious that I'd rather not have her touch me. "I know what to do. How to get into the mine."

"You do?" She leaned toward me, that same easy smile on her face that made me feel like she already knew what I was going to say. "How?"

"It's not a matter of sneaking in at all." The excitement was brewing inside of me. I finally had a plan. I could finally take some action. I smiled back at her for maybe the first time since we'd met. "I'm going to walk right in. And Luthair's going to be the one to put me there."

The light was still on in Harbin's second-floor room when I arrived that night. It cast a dull orange glow on the overgrown garden below, a glow I was careful to avoid as I picked up a couple of small stones, which were in no short supply. I tossed the first one, and it glanced off of the window pane. A couple of breaths later, I threw the second, then the third. It took five pebbles before I saw movement inside and heard the glass slide open.

Harbin's head appeared, a dark shadow against the light. "Frida?"

I stepped into the light. "Come to the wharf with me." It was the best place I could think of to get drunk and pick a fight. I couldn't do it at the Gold Mine. Erik and Estrid would haul me away before I could get a punch in. But every night, the sailors and dock-workers who hadn't sailed out that day gathered on the ships and played cards and drank ale from unclaimed casks. It was known to get rowdy. A fight there would be commonplace.

"The wharf?" Harbin scratched his head and looked up and

down the street as if searching for my accomplices. "Why are you going to the wharf?"

I jingled my purse, full of a couple pennies Gerves gave me for putting to rights the dining room after the fight and washing the night's dishes. "I'm feeling lucky."

"That would be a change." Harbin shut the window. The light in his room extinguished, and a few moments later, the front door to the rooming house creaked slowly open. He emerged dressed in loose, dark clothes, still strapping on his sword belt as he fell into step beside me.

We walked to the wharf on the road lit only by the eerie blue light of Gleet that cast everything in strange relief, like being underwater.

When we were beyond the limits of town, Harbin turned to me. "Maybe now you'll tell me the real reason we're going to the wharf."

I shrugged. "I told you."

"A couple pennies burning a hole in your purse? I don't think so."

"What do you mean?"

"For as long as I've known you, you've saved every coin that has passed through your fingertips, each one bringing you a bit closer to escaping Bruhier." He took a couple steps ahead and turned around, walking backward in front of me. "No, whatever we're doing, you've got a plan. And I want to know what it is before I get involved. And more likely than not, seriously injured."

"Fine." I laughed and stopped walking.

He leaned in close.

Maybe a little too close, but at least I could whisper this way. "I'm going to go play some cards, drink some ale, throw some punches, and get myself arrested."

He furrowed his brow. "What? Why? That makes even less sense."

So I told him everything—about Tsarra Trisfina and Arun Phina and their promise to get us home. When I finished, we stood on the edge of the hill that led to the wharf. Lanterns burned on ships' decks, and the sounds of music and laughter drifted up to us.

"I may never see you again after tonight," Harbin said suddenly. "If you free the elf and escape the mine."

A big if, to be sure. I glanced over at him. "Don't be silly. You're a sailor and I'm an adventurer. Our paths will cross again if they're meant to."

This late, there was no one operating the lift so we had to take the path down, a switchback staircase carved into the stone, worn slick from use over the years. The iron railing was slippery with sea spray, but I held on tight, following Harbin to the wooden docks below.

We boarded the *Gem*, where Harbin was greeted heartily by his crewmates and I was mostly ignored, which was fine by me. The card table was set up on the main deck, and there was a crowd around it, but only a few men were sitting. Most I didn't recognize, but then my eyes fell on one who looked even more out of place than I did. And his female companion.

Aysche Luthair and her on-again, off-again beau, Jesper Chauzin. Around them, a group of Jesper's friends gathered, distinguishable by their clean gold-trimmed tunics and polished boots.

This was even better than I could have imagined.

As I pulled out one of the empty chairs and took a seat, Jesper's eyes met mine. He nudged Aysche, who stood behind him, and even though I looked quickly away, I felt the moment she found me sitting at the card table and fought to keep a smile off my face.

Jesper was Stephan Luthair's lieutenant, his second-in-command. And he hated me just as much as his employer did. He hated anyone who didn't fall in line and do as they're told.

He had a sour expression on a head that was too small for the rest of him. His hair was always greased into place, and his face was plagued with acne because of it. Aysche didn't mind, of course—he had money and power. What more could a girl want?

Harbin took the seat beside me, placing two mugs of ale on the table between us.

"I see where this is going." He lifted his drink to his lips. He may not have lived in Barepost full time, but he knew the politics all the same. Besides, he'd grown up with Aysche and Jesper, and I didn't think he would mind if they got their asses kicked.

"Just keep them coming," I said through gritted teeth.

"What is she doing here?" Aysche asked loudly enough that most of the activity around the table stopped.

The dealer—a man from town I recognized but didn't know by name—gave the cards one last shuffle and then banged them on the table. He glanced at me and then away, his demeanor unconcerned, but I knew he also didn't likely want to lose Jesper's money. "The Svand? Is she a cheat?"

Aysche huffed. "Probably."

He looked at me again. "Are you a cheat?"

I took a long swing of the ale and wiped my mouth on my sleeve. It was quiet enough that I could hear the water slapping against the ship's hull. "No. I've never actually played before." It wasn't a lie, not really. Estrid and Erik had never let me play, but I'd watched so many of their games that I knew what I was doing.

The dealer's eyes lit up. "She's fine to stay."

"If she stays, then I'm leaving." Aysche stood, smoothing down her yellow skirts. "Come on, Jesper."

Instead of glaring at me, Jesper was looking longingly at the card table. "But—"

I stole Harbin's mug and drained it, and then pushed myself

to my feet, bracing my hands on the table as my head spun. "You afraid, Luthair?"

She gathered herself up and did her best to look down her nose at me in spite of the fact that I towered over her. "Yes. We should all fear monsters."

"Funny how sometimes the worst monsters wear the prettiest faces."

The insult hit home.

"Now look here, D'ahvol." Jesper stood, coming between Aysche and me. "You can't just—"

"Trash!" Aysche shouted, interrupting her own defender. "What right do you have to even address me? You and your family are no better than my uncle's slaves."

Slaves? The flush that rose in my cheeks had nothing to do with the ale that was working its way through my system.

Harbin rose to his feet beside me.

"Everyone, just calm down." The dealer pushed his chair away from the table, out of the line of fire.

"I suggest you leave immediately, D'ahvol, or I'll be forced to call the governor." Jesper wagged a finger at me, keeping his other hand on Aysche's shoulder.

"I'm counting on it." My fist connected with his nose with a satisfying crunch. The blow sent him stumbling back a step until his legs hit the chair, and he collapsed onto it, holding his face in his hands.

"She hit me," he wailed, his voice even more annoying than normal, muffled and high-pitched.

I shook out my hand and smiled at him.

One of the other boys with Jesper launched himself over the table, taking a valiant leap that knocked me flat beneath him. His weight was crushing but only briefly. Harbin hefted him off of me, and the two of them went scrambling after each other across the deck. I pushed to my feet and took in the chaos around me.

The men and women of the *Gem* didn't need much of a reason to brawl with the uppity group that had come with Jesper and Aysche, and they were doing a fine job of it. Seemingly out of nowhere, a man in sailor's garb flew across the card table, sending the table itself toppling to the floor. He stood, brushed himself off, and ran back into the melee, laughing with glee.

Jesper had had enough time to recover by now. He cleared the distance between us in two steps, and I met him just as eagerly, blocking his first swing with my arm and coming up underneath with an uppercut to his gut. Grabbing his stomach, he doubled over, and I brought my knee up to meet his face. His hands shot out and grabbed my thigh, pulling me off-balance and sending me toppling back against the deck, my hands slamming against the rough wood. I swiped my legs at him, catching him around the ankles and pulling him down with me.

We grappled for a moment there on the deck, each of us winning and then losing the advantage, rolling and scrabbling, hands blindly grasping for purchase against each other's faces. He dug a thumb into one of my eyes, and I shrieked and rolled, straddling him, one of my hands wrapped around his neck.

"Do you know how many times I've wanted to do this?" I didn't expect an answer. His hands were on my wrist, trying to tug me away. I wasn't squeezing hard, not really. I didn't want to kill him and spend the *rest* of my life in the mine. I just needed a little bruising to show for my efforts.

When he bucked his hips, I let go, sliding off of him and scrambling to my feet, ready to continue our battle until I felt the tip of something cold against the back of my neck. I raised my hands in surrender and slowly turned to find a guard in black uniform, his sword leveled at my face.

Aysche stood beside him, a smug smile on her lips, her yellow dress neat and clean.

I bared my teeth at her.

"Why am I not surprised to find you here, Svand?" The guard seemed to know who I was, though I had never seen him before. Or if I had, I didn't remember him. He looked just like every other guard in Barepost. Our reputation really had grown.

I grinned at him in response, my chest heaving from the excitement.

"Take her weapons."

Someone else stepped forward and removed my ax and my sword from their sheaths at my sides. I hadn't even drawn them in the excitement.

I chanced a look around and saw that several sailors were held as I was. I didn't see Harbin among them, but none of Jesper's friends were under arrest. They were all broken and bloody, nursing their wounds. Jesper was no exception. He sat with his head tilted back, pinching the bridge of his bleeding nose. I didn't even realize I had his blood on my hands until that moment when I looked down at the red smears on my fingers and arms.

Aysche ignored Jesper and clung to the guard holding me at sword-point. She turned a cold gaze on me. "My uncle won't stand for this." Her voice carried a healthy dose of bravado, which was a surprising amount for someone who'd been scared witless only moments before. "You'll pay this time, Svand. Mark my words."

Another guard bound my hands before the sword was lowered.

I was the first one marched off the ship and up the narrow path to the plateau. Up and up we went, past the main strip, which was mostly dark, and onto the cobbled street that led up the mountainside to Luthair's residence. Lights burned in all of his windows as if he thought leaving the lamps on all night would scare away the beasts. If Aysche was right, though, he was opening his door to one right now.

My first thought, when I saw him standing in the light of his open door was that he looked tired. There were dark circles under his eyes, and his robe and hair were rumpled. In spite of this, he surveyed me and the rest of the fighters as coolly as ever.

"Take them to the inner barracks." His eyes found me. "Except for Ms. Svand. She and I have much to discuss."

I ground my teeth, resisting the urge to argue. When everyone else had left, my guard and I entered.

Luthair closed the door behind us with an ominous click that made me suddenly desperate to leave.

I turned my eyes to the giant window on the far wall but saw only my own reflection. "I'll do my time." I couldn't stand his silent contemplation any longer. "I won't fight you."

He smiled, a look that sent chills down my spine, a look that told me he knew exactly what I wanted and that he wasn't going to give it to me. Not without something in exchange. He gestured to the guard behind me, a small twitch of his hand, but before I could turn to see what was happening, something slammed against the back of my head with a sickening thud. My vision went black, and I fought to stay on my feet, but it was useless. As I fell, toppling over like a blazetaur with no stinger, I gave into the darkness and knew no more.

CHAPTER 7

I balanced on the very edge of the rock, my toes digging into the mossy ground. Below me, waves crashed against the cliff of Bor'sur, trying and failing to topple the city that dared to reach into the sky. It was my favorite place, here, on the edge of the world. It felt like I could, at any moment, spread my wings and fly.

Behind me, my father's voice. "Look up, my star. Don't forget to look up."

I tilted my head back, and the whole sky opened up to me, so black it was almost blue, thousands and thousands of stars clustered together, winking back at me.

"They are the spirits of our ancestors, the ones who died fighting Dag'draath in the Dark War. They have blessed you, my star, and will always be there to guide you. Never forget to look up."

I touched a finger to the mark beside my eye and thought of the D'ahvol who came before me, who faced down the God of Darkness himself and fought for Onen Suun. Fought to keep the world from plunging into the darkness. I could only hope to someday be as brave as them, to be worthy of their blessing.

Behind me, my father smelled of spices and leather and smoke. I breathed in deep and turned to him, only to find no one there. No one *and nothing. Where the lights of Bor'sur should have been was only black shadow, dark tendrils climbing the cliff, reaching for me. Overhead, the stars were blinking out, one by one.*

I JERKED INTO CONSCIOUSNESS, my eyes opening onto an unfamiliar room bathed in light. At first, it was a welcome relief not to be facing down the sentient darkness of my dream, but then the memory of the night before came rushing back.

The fight, the guards, Luthair and his sly grin.

I slowly pushed myself to sitting, taking in my surroundings. Stone walls and red drapes, a heavy wooden door across from me, and floor-to-ceiling windows on the eastern wall. I wasn't in any normal holding cell at all. I was still in Luthair's estate. It was the only building in town with this kind of view.

The thick quilt slipped down as I moved, and I yelped, surprised to find myself dressed in only a thin muslin shirt two sizes too big. When I stood, I clutched at the quilt, wrapping it around me. It was a poor excuse for my usual armor but certainly better than being half-naked.

Across the room, a basin of steaming water sat on the dresser, waiting for me. It unnerved me to realize someone had been in here, had stripped me of my clothes, and had seen me sleeping. They could have killed me, and I would have been none the wiser. Even worse, it could have been Luthair, gazing down at me while I was at my most vulnerable, eyes on my naked body. The thought sent chills down my spine that had nothing to do with the fresh air slipping in through the window panes.

The looking glass over the basin revealed more disturbing details. My face and hands and every other part of me had been scrubbed clean while I slept, and my hair had been washed and combed. It hung light and golden around my flushed face. My head throbbed, but if there'd been any blood from the impact, it had been washed away. All that was left was a tender lump at the back of my skull.

Securing the blanket around me with a knot, I scrubbed my hands in the warm water and splashed my face, clearing the sleep from my eyes. I needed to be awake to face Luthair when he arrived, whatever the reason for this lavish and unwelcome attention.

It was then that I spotted, over my shoulder in the mirror, my clothes folded neatly on a trunk at the foot of the bed. I dried my hands and picked them up, examining the clean clothes, smooth leather, and shining buckles. They'd been freshly laundered, and the leather armor oiled. As I slipped them on, it occurred to me that I hadn't been this clean in three years or more, certainly not since leaving the Western March. The only things missing were my weapons. The sword and its sheath were nowhere to be seen, and neither was my treasured ax. I swore to Oya, the Goddess of War, that I would strike Luthair down with my bare hands if he didn't return it to me before I left this island.

Near the hearth was a table set with a platter of cold break-fast foods—soft-boiled eggs, poached salmon, soft cheeses, and buttered toast. A far cry from Gerves's leftover stews. I could see why Luthair had turned his nose up at the innkeeper's offer-ings. Even though I ate my fill, I wondered what Luthair was playing at.

It wasn't the first time he'd made an attempt to show me his softer side, to try to convince me he was anything less than a brute and a bully. He'd been decent at first, even kind at times, giving me and my sister food and shelter while the healer looked after our brother. But as I knew now, nothing Luthair did was for free. I'd heard Erik and Estrid once, back when Erik was still bedridden.

"He'll release me of my debt if we give her to him," Erik had said.

Estrid had made a low growl in her throat. "He wants to add her to his collection of pretty things. Lock her up in his tower on the mountain."

"She could have a good life here."

Here? I'd thought, realizing with a start that they were talking about me, discussing my future as if I had no say in it at all. Not likely. I had never been the kind of girl who cared for finery and comfort.

"Not the life she wants," Estrid answered for me.

"She doesn't know what she wants!" Erik grew louder, and I could hear Estrid murmuring gently to soothe him. "Look at what I've gotten her into on this, our first excursion."

"The trip was my idea, so if anyone has gotten her into this, it's me. No one blames you, but mark my words. If you sell her to this governor, she will never forgive you, and neither will I."

I hadn't really understood then, but I did now. Luthair had offered to release my brother from his life-debt in exchange for my hand in marriage. I was torn on the idea, bothered mostly by the fact that my siblings hadn't even talked to me about it. But it had also been a chance for me to do something unselfish, something to save them for a change. On the other hand, I could barely stomach the idea of life here as the Lady Luthair. It was probably just as well that they'd made the decision for me.

Was that what this was now? Did Luthair think my affection could be won with comfort and good food? That I would marry him to avoid having to do time in the mines? If so, he was sorely mistaken. No, there was no amount of finery that would cause me to forgive the governor and what he'd put us through these last few years. Nothing he could say that would convince me to give up the rest of my life to him.

After I ate and still, no one had come, I found myself contemplating the door. There was only one in the room and it was shut tight. No amount of tugging moved it, and I picked at the iron lock to no avail. The window was even more hopeless, though the view was magnificent. Even if I could get it open, there was the straight drop down into Barepost to contend with.

Hours passed, the sun climbing higher into the sky. I had nothing better to do than watch it, my hands pressed to the glass, feeling it grow warmer. After midday, when the sun was no longer visible, I took a thin butter knife from the table and began to work at the wooden window frame, leveraging the knife against the wall and attempting to pry the wood away to free the glass. I didn't know what I would do if it worked except breathe fresh air. All this time indoors was driving me mad, but I wasn't an avian who could just fly down the mountain, after all.

I had just popped a nail from the wall when the door behind me opened. I wheeled around, knife in hand, holding it before me as if it were a great sword.

Luthair stood in the open doorway, an amused smirk on his face. He looked like his usual self—well rested and groomed and smug. "Well, you do clean up nicely. I always expected as much, but it's good to have confirmation."

I was nearly on top of him, the butter knife inches from his throat, when a guard caught me up, whirling me around and trapping my arms behind my back and knocking the knife to the floor. I hadn't seen him there or he wouldn't have been able to get the better of me. Panting, I jerked my arms just to keep him on his toes.

"Let her go," Luthair said with a dismissive flick of his hand.

The guard did, and I stumbled away.

A serving girl came in behind them, wheeling a cart loaded with more food. My stomach growled greedily. I'd eaten more in one day than I had in the last week, and I still longed for more. She cleared the breakfast dishes and replaced them with two empty dinner plates. When she and the guard left, shutting the door behind them, Luthair took a seat at the table, his back to me, wholly unconcerned for his safety. I eyed the door, wondering if I could make a break for it.

"Don't bother," Luthair said without even looking at me. "It's locked, and there is a guard on the other side if you do somehow manage to muscle your way out. Come, have a seat. We should talk."

Everything inside of me fought against obeying him, but an even bigger part of me knew never to turn down a meal. I sat and began heaping my plate high with roast pork and vegetables and steaming dinner rolls.

He watched, his disgust at my manners plain on his face, and then shrugged, reaching for a dinner roll before I managed to eat them all. "What did you make of the Lady Trisfina and her sob story?"

I inhaled sharply, nearly choking on a pea. I coughed and took a gulp of water from the wooden cup set before my plate. "Who?"

"Quite the tale, isn't it? An elf family in ruin. The only man who can save them locked away in the deepest bowels of a prison mine by a tyrant governor. Lovers, destined for doom." The flat tone of his voice made it obvious he did not think much of the tale.

That was surprising. I don't know how he knew, or how much he knew, but I wouldn't give anything away. "I don't know what you're talking about."

"Ah, so you're not going to try to free Arun Phina? What a relief. He's become a huge asset in the mine, even more so than the one he bargained for. Leader of his group, even. I would hate to lose him."

He knew. He knew everything. How was that possible?

Luthair chewed his food meticulously, giving me time to think, and then waved his knife in the air as if fanning away an unpleasant smell. "I'm not here to argue with you, though. I'm here to bargain with you. There are other options. Better options."

"Better than what?" This should be good.

"Better than enslaving yourself to an elf family. You know they keep slaves, right? Don't think your elf blood will help you. To them, the D'ahvol are no better than us lowly humans." His words dripped with contempt, which I found strange considering he had basically enslaved me and my siblings without a second thought.

"The D'ahvol are no one's slaves." It was the truth. We were a fierce people, bred to fight and love ferociously, but always independently. Never at anyone else's beck and call.

He looked away, suddenly very interested in his food. "You could be . . . something else. You could help me govern Barepost at my side. You would never owe anyone anything ever again."

I would sooner wrestle with a trithon. "The only bargain I'm interested in is you releasing us of Erik's life-debt and letting us leave Barepost. All three of us."

He dabbed the corners of his mouth with a napkin and took a sip of wine before responding. "Out of the question. A day will come soon when I will need the Svands for more than just pest control. But . . . perhaps I don't need all of them. I'm willing to offer you your freedom if you will abandon your quest to free Arun Phina. Do not start that war in my city. Do not make me do things that the people will regret."

"What about Erik and Estrid?"

"Just you." He shook his head. "The *Gem* sails tomorrow for Cliffside. You can be on that ship if you agree."

For one shameful moment, I allowed myself to imagine it. The open sea, the wind on my face, Bruhier nothing but a speck in the distance. The dark forests of the lowlands and the towering spires of the elven city of Cliffside rising on the horizon. But I would be alone, and to leave without my siblings would be shameful. There would be nowhere I could go to escape that shame and loneliness.

"I won't leave them." I met his gaze. "I can't."

Luthair resumed eating, his plate nearly clean. "Well," he said between bites, "I suppose it's to the mines with you, then. Three days for brawling. Three days to really think it over."

"I don't have to think it over." Three days to free Arun Phina and escape Barepost. I'd made a promise to Tsarra Trisfina and a promise to myself. I would get us off of this island.

"I suppose you'll meet Arun Phina in the mines and that you'll try to free him, but know this. If I lose him, I will have to replace him." He looked thoughtful and then smiled at me. "Erik would make an excellent alternative. I would be glad to allow him to serve out the rest of the elf's life sentence. And you and I both know that Erik will do it if I ask."

He wasn't wrong. Whether he'd known what he was doing when he'd sent that team down the mountain for us three years ago and ordered his healer to do whatever it took to revive Erik, I'd never know. But the fact of the matter was, Luthair had saved Erik's life, and in return, won himself a D'ahvol life-debt. Life-debts were sacred to my people. To break them meant never joining my ancestors in the sky, and instead, toiling for an eternity in the depths of Ash'gar. I had no doubt that Luthair would force Erik into the mines. How would I ever live with myself then?

But I also had no doubt that I could free Arun Phina, and I had my own promise to keep now. Not a life-debt, but I'd given my word to Tsarra Trisfina, and I intended to keep it.

Luthair spoke little after that, as if recognizing a lost cause when he saw one. After we ate, the same serving girl cleared the plates, and Luthair left with her, locking me in my luxurious cell.

"Enjoy it while you can," he said on his way out. "You'll find that the mines are not so accommodating."

But I couldn't enjoy it. The bed was too soft and the windows too bright, even here beneath the veil of clouds. Aupra and Gleet were both out tonight, bathing the room in their eerie blue and white lights. My dream from the night before came back to me in bits and pieces, but the clouds were too thick for any stars to shine through. It was easy to feel like I'd been forgotten by my ancestors, abandoned on this horrible island, left to my own dark fate.

CHAPTER 8

The next morning, I was roused from a restless sleep before the dawn by rough hands dragging the covers away and pulling me to my feet. The woman was short and chubby, with round cheeks and curled silver hair. When I asked who she was, she told me to call her Missus and to stop asking so many questions. After my shirt was on, I reached for my leather armor.

Missus yanked it away. "No armor or weapons," she croaked. "Governor's orders."

Of course. He would send me into the mines with nothing but the clothes on my back. It would make escaping with Arun Phina harder, but I enjoyed a good challenge. My ax, though—I would have to come back for it. I couldn't leave that piece of me behind.

I didn't see Luthair again as I was marched out of his estate and joined the other miners on their trek up the mountain. I drew some looks—understandable with my shackles and guards —but most people were so absorbed in their own misery that they ignored me.

"Frida!"

I turned to the voice. Erik was there with Estrid and Harbin, who had his pack on and looked ready to sail out on the Gem. A rope of dead fish hung on his belt, an offering to Sirsir, the god of mariners, for a safe passage.

"What did you do?" Erik asked, though I was sure Harbin had told him. He reached for me, and one of the guards pushed him back. He growled, but Estrid put a hand on his arm.

"Three days," I said. "Be ready. Stay away from the governor."

It was all I had a chance to say as we reached the mountain path and began to climb, each person looping a rope through a metal hook on their belt. I didn't have one, but my guards did, and they secured me between them for the duration of the climb.

When we made it to the mine entrance about halfway up the cliff, we filed one by one inside the mine. It was a squat hole in the mountainside braced by massive wooden beams. Most of the day's workers went into a tunnel on the right lined with lamps that shone on a wooden staircase leading gently downhill, but my guards tugged me left toward a set of iron tracks and a wooden cart.

"You're in the old tunnels," one of them said.

One of the only things I knew about the mines was that the original entrance was near the base of the mountain, which meant the old tunnels ran deep below the surface. I remembered Luthair saying that Arun Phina was in the bowels of the mine. Did the man really have the bravado to assign me to the same position as the very man he knew I was trying to free?

The cart only had room for me and one of my guards, so we piled in, the guard sitting behind the wheel, one hand on the brake lever. The other guard gave us a push, and we slid down the track, picking up speed as we descended. Even with my heart in my throat and my stomach flip-flopping, I tried to keep my eyes open to memorize our path and to search for entrances and exits and hiding places. I saw nothing of use, and a few minutes into our descent, completely lost my sense of direction. There were times when the tunnel became so narrow and the ceiling so low that I had to duck my head for fear of it being lobbed off before I even had a chance to see what Arun Phina looked like.

As the track finally leveled out, the guard pulled on the brake, coming to a smooth stop in a depot of sorts.

"Done that before, have you?" I asked him, my legs shaking as I stood and spilled myself over the edge of the cart onto solid ground.

"Only every time I have to bring one of you assholes down here," he said gruffly, his bushy mustache moving more than his mouth when he spoke.

The depot was a tall, round cavern with several adjoining tunnels leading off in different directions, like the spokes on a wheel. To my left looked to be the mess hall, a wide, open space lined with long tables and benches. To my right, dark, quiet tunnels. Living quarters, maybe? There was no obvious way out except for the way we'd come. Even the ventilation shafts, tiny holes set high in the roof, were far too small for a person of any substantial size to squeeze through.

"D'ahvol!" a man's voice shouted, echoing across the cavern. Then, in my own language of Ahvoli, he said, "It has been a long time since I have seen one of my own."

I couldn't believe it. Another D'ahvol in Barepost. The voice belonged to a towering, barrel-chested man whose long, narrow nose and squinted eyes made him look more like a mole than a person. But his size and his fair skin gave him away for what he was, no matter how unlikely it was to find him here.

"Foreman Haklang," the guard said, "in Iynian, if you please."

Haklang smiled wide, baring crooked, yellow teeth, and clapped the guard on the shoulder with a force that could have felled a lesser man. "Oh, yes, I please," he said in Iynian, the common language spoken in nearly all countries. "I always please."

The guard turned to me, rubbing his shoulder. "This is the foreman. Down here, his word is law. For the next three days, you do as you're told." He turned to Haklang. "No special treatment just because she's D'ahvol."

"Never." Haklang continued to smile.

I liked this one.

The guard left, activating a pulley system on the track that dragged the cart back to the entrance.

Haklang motioned for me to follow him. He outfitted me with the belt all the miners wore with metal hooks and holsters full of pickaxes and hammers, and a helmet that was slightly too big, the visor drooping down over my eyes.

We entered a mineshaft, the only one with any lanterns lighting the stone walls, and used hooks and ropes to secure ourselves as we descended. I could hear the distant echo of hammers and men's voices but couldn't see anyone yet.

"So, tell me, D'ahvol," he said, slipping back into Ahvoli, I thought for the sheer pleasure of it. "How do you find yourself here?"

I shrugged, the movement causing me to slip.

He caught me with a hand on my arm and showed me how to use the ropes, not unfastening one until the other was secure. This was . . . harder than it looked.

"Looking for adventure. Finding only trouble and monsters to slay for a pittance." The Ahvoli words felt strange on my tongue, but I slipped easily into my native language. It felt like coming home.

"Ah," Haklang said, as if it made all the sense in the world. "I, too, came to slay monsters and wound up corralling them here, instead."

"Why do you stay?" I wondered if he was perhaps one of the criminals bound to the mines or if he was here voluntarily.

"The pay is good." He navigated a particularly steep decline and then reached back to help me. "Governor Luthair is fair. And I have found at my age that sometimes safety and security are preferable to adventure and fame."

I did not voice my disbelief because that was when the tunnel narrowed, and the rest of the miners came into view. The mineshaft was packed with men, all of them, I realized, likely criminals. They didn't look like criminals down here, though. They looked like tired, underfed, defeated men working to survive. Their clothes hung off of skinny frames, and most of their arms seemed barely strong enough to hold a hammer.

"We've been working at this seam of coal for years," Haklang said. "I expect there are still years of work ahead of us."

We were both ducking, and I could reach from one side of the tunnel to the other without moving. It felt like the whole world was going to cave in on me.

No one else seemed affected, slouched and crowded as they were. Some men hammered at the stone wall, tossing shining, black rocks into wagons. Other men moved the wagons to the belts that would convey the rocks to the waiting carts, while still others sorted out the bits of rock and debris. The carts would transport the coal to the surface, where it could be sold to residents of Barepost to power their lamps and stoves, or loaded onto ships and sold to other colonies on Bruhier or even other countries. Coal was not Luthair's most lucrative export, but it might have been the most abundant. And watching over it all were dozens of guards in uniform, black masks covering the bottom halves of their faces.

Down here, escape seemed even more impossible than it had in the cart on the way in. There was no natural light seeping in, no unexplored or unattended offshoot that would miraculously lead to the outside world. It was a maze of dark, narrow tunnels that led ever downward. The world beyond the mines had disappeared. I understood now why this was the worst punishment imaginable for criminals on Barepost.

A clamoring noise interrupted the monotonous sound of hammers and axes striking stone.

Haklang rushed forward.

I followed, my head ducked low and my knees bent to make me fit in the mineshaft. There was a figure sprawled on the ground, his long, grey hair fanned around his head.

"Bertol." Haklang hurried toward the man but stopped short as someone else came into view.

A guard stepped forward and swung a short whip at the man. The strap cracked against the old man's back. "Get to work."

The old man groaned and tried to push to his feet. Another lash fell, this one opening a gash in the white shirt. Blood stained the fabric. I started to move forward but Haklang stopped me, his arm across my shoulders. I looked at him in disbelief. Was he going to do nothing? Was he going to stand there and watch an old man be beaten to death?

"Bertol," Haklang said again, this time loud enough for the man to hear. "Get up, Bertol. There is work to be done."

Another crack of the whip, but this time, the strap fell across a broad, muscled arm.

"Oh, Yina, help us," Haklang said under his breath, beseeching the Guardian for assistance.

The muscled arm snatched the whip from the guard and tossed it aside.

The guard shouted something, but the man attached to the arm crouched down over Bertol, ignoring the guard. He was as tall and wide as Haklang, but he had a brown tint to his skin and long black hair that was pulled back with a leather thong at the nape of his neck. His muscled back strained against his shirt, which was soaked through with sweat and coal dust, but his ears were what drew my attention. The tops of them tapered into sharp points, belying his elven heritage.

This had to be Arun Phina.

"You will suffer for this, elf." The guard was trying to push his way to them, but a small crowd had gathered to watch.

Arun Phina didn't seem fazed by the threats. He rolled the old man over. Haklang took tentative steps toward them. I followed, not sure what I was supposed to do. This was the man I'd come to rescue. Do? Don't? He certainly looked capable.

Arun grunted, kneeling beside Bertol and propping him up. "Was it another attack?"

Bertol groaned in response.

"Get him up," Haklang said. "I'll take him."

"Stand aside." The guard had muscled his way to us now.

I turned to him, drawing myself up as best as I could, blocking his view of Bertol.

"Hi," I said. "I'm Frida. I'm new here." I held out my hand for him to shake it.

He looked at it as if it were diseased. "Move, D'ahvol."

"Can you show me where to go?" I put a hand on his shoulder, trying to turn him away. "They haven't shown me my post yet."

He knocked my hand away. "Move, or it will be your turn at the end of the whip."

"Which end?"

He grabbed my wrist and dragged me forward. Still unused to being hunched over, I wasn't able to get my balance back, so I toppled forward, hitting the stone hard with my bare hands.

But when he'd gotten past me, Haklang and Bertol were nowhere to be seen.

Arun Phina knelt there with the whip in his hand. "I believe this belongs to you." He offered the handle to the guard.

The guard snatched it from him. I thought he might hit him,

but then he tucked the whip into a hook on his belt. "Half rations for the rest of the day."

When he returned to his post and the rest of the miners had resumed their work, I turned to Arun Phina. "I—"

"You can take over for Bertol for the rest of the day," he interrupted. His face held none of its former easy amusement. It was straight and serious.

"Oh," I answered, taken aback. "I can do that."

Using less than three words, he showed me how to sort debris from the coal before transferring it to the carts, and then left me to my work. The whole time, I'd wanted to tell him about Tsarra Trisfina and my mission, but he'd made it clear that I wasn't to speak, only listen and work. I wanted to resent him, but I couldn't, not after seeing what he'd done for Bertol.

At what I assumed was midday, a boy of about ten years brought around packs of seeds and nuts with strips of dried meat for lunch. He was dark-haired and skinny, his face and clothes filthy and his feet bare. One of his eyes was covered with a black patch on which someone had drawn a Jolly Roger.

"You're Frida." He handed me my package. It wasn't a question, more like a confirmation.

"I am." I leaned on the edge of the cart, peeking inside the pack. Most of the other miners had stopped to take a break, too, and the sound of hammering had been replaced by the sound of murmured conversation.

Arun was nearby, speaking to some other young men and ignoring me, his pack of food noticeably smaller than everyone else's. Half rations, I supposed.

"And you are?"

"I'm Xalph. My da's Haklang." He stood there, watching me expectantly.

"Is that so?" I gnawed at the strip of meat, thinking. "And your mom?"

He shrugged. "Da says my ma was Lark."

I nodded at him as if it were an entirely possible idea for him to be born from the Goddess of Mischief. Instead, Haklang's presence here suddenly made a lot more sense. I suspected he'd gotten some Barepost woman with child years ago in the course of his adventuring and been forced by honor and duty to stay, taking a job in the mines to support his unexpected family. I wondered if she'd left as my own mother had, and I felt a tenderness in my heart toward this boy. "I take it you're particularly mischievous, then?"

"Da says so, and Da's always right."

I offered him a nut. "Is he?"

He took it, crunching down on it "Well, Da says so."

I laughed.

Xalph beamed at me.

I got the feeling he didn't get much attention down here. What would it be like to be a child of the mines, raised in the dark by criminals? "Can I ask what happened to your eye?"

"Mining accident." Xalph puffed his chest up like this was some badge of honor, something to be proud of. He pulled up his pant leg then and showed me how one of his ankles was twisted as if it had broken and never healed right. "A tunnel collapsed on me when I was just a lad."

"And what are you now? An old man?"

His face grew serious. "I'd say anyone that's been crushed beneath a mountain and lived to tell it cannot be called a lad anymore."

I had no response to that, so I just offered him another nut.

He took it, considering me while he chewed. "I like you, so I'm going to tell you something secret. The governor has me spy on people sometimes for extra coin. He came this morning and told me to keep a special eye on you." He pointed to his one good eye and smiled, baring small yellow teeth at me.

I wasn't surprised to know that Luthair was watching me,

but I thought it was beneath even him to use a child to do it. "What are you supposed to tell him?"

He shrugged his bony shoulders. "Everything you do."

"Well, you can tell him all about my sorting abilities." I motioned to the nearly-full cart behind me.

"I won't tell him anything. But will you tell me what kind of trouble we're about to get into?"

Over his head, my eyes found Arun Phina. "The fun kind." I wasn't entirely sure I was telling the truth.

CHAPTER 9

The sorting work wasn't hard, but it was tedious. Time crawled without the sun to mark the hours. I was glad when the bell finally rang and the miners began filing back toward the depot. Even that was slow-going, with everyone worn-out from the day's work.

Dinner was a lumpy slop that made Gerves's stew look good and yesterday's luxurious meals like a distant dream. But I was starving and had no problem lowering my standards. I ate it alone at the end of one of the long tables, mostly ignored by the others who seemed to know I didn't fit in with them.

When I was nearly done and considering licking the bowl, Haklang appeared at the mouth of a tunnel near the back of the dining hall. "Group A to the springs," he announced.

A group of men stood, including Arun Phina, and trailed into the tunnel after a guard. At the last minute, Arun turned to me.

"You're with us."

I tried not to look too eager as I dumped my bowl in the wash bin and scurried after them.

Haklang led us through a tunnel, the air growing warmer as

we walked. We emerged into another large cavern lit by rows of blackened torches on the walls. Here, rocks seemed to drip from the ceiling, making columns that dipped into a clear blue pool. Steam rose from the water, and water droplets gathered on the ceiling.

"The governor started letting us have baths after complaints about our working conditions." Arun appeared beside me.

"Oh." So he was talking to me now. "Very generous, that governor."

Arun was already moving up in the line.

So just keeping everyone informed. How . . . thoughtful.

A guard handed each of us a towel, and several of the men began to strip in the main cavern. I wanted nothing more than to plunge myself in the hot water and rinse off the grime of the day, but I wouldn't do it with an audience.

I walked around the spring to a series of small caves and ducked inside one of the mouths, finding my own private pool. Keeping my clothes on, I lowered myself into the water. It was scalding hot, but I didn't mind. Crouching in the pool, my feet slipping on the slick rocks, I removed my shirt and pants and underthings, and scrubbed them beneath the water. Then I laid them on a hot rock nearby to dry before turning my attention to my dusty skin and hair. Holding my breath, I sank to the bottom and ran my fingers through my hair, glad I wore it fairly short even if it wasn't the style. Most of the women in Barepost kept their hair in long braids down their backs. Even men typically wore it at least to their shoulders.

I stayed there for as long as I could stand, until my lungs strained against my chest for breath. Pushing off the bottom, I burst through the surface, inhaling the warm, wet air in the cavern.

"Oh," came a man's voice.

Startled, I turned to see Arun Phina standing in the mouth of the cave, his eyes resolutely on mine, as if he knew that to drop them to any other part of my body would mean his certain death.

Even still, I crossed my arms over my chest, feeling my cheeks flush. The D'ahvol were not necessarily a modest people, but I still didn't want to go around baring myself to the first handsome elf I met.

"I didn't know where you'd gone . . ."

"Well, here I am."

His wet hair dripped onto his shoulders, darkening his white shirt. "Here you are." He cleared his throat and turned around. "Our time is about up. We have to clear out."

"I'm coming. Just give me a minute to . . ." I waved a hand at my clothes even though he wasn't looking at me anymore.

"Yes. Sure, of course." His hand jerked as if he wanted to say something else, and then he left.

If I thought I could get away with it, I would have sunk to the bottom of the spring and never come back up. Instead, I made myself get out and towel off. I dressed in my damp but clean clothes and made my way out to the main cavern where the rest of my group was waiting for me.

Arun Phina, whose cheeks I thought were a little pink, did not make eye contact with me as we followed our guard escort away from the springs.

This time, we were led to the sleeping quarters, which was really a series of small caverns packed with cots, some of them layered on top of each other in bunks. The men climbed into their cots happily and turned off their bedside lanterns, most seeming to fall into an easy sleep belied by their loud, rumbling snores. I found an empty cot on the far wall and sat on its edge, feeling too restless to really sleep. My thoughts were with Xalph and Haklang and Arun Phina, all of them trapped here for different reasons, serving the same sentence. Surely someone would wither and die down here, without the sun and the sea and the sky.

"Your thoughts are so loud, I cannot sleep," said a man's voice.

I looked up and saw Arun Phina standing over me. His hair had dried in a frizzy halo around his head, once again hiding his ears. He almost looked like any other prisoner.

"Same here," I said, that same blasted flush creeping up my neck.

"It's hardest in the beginning. May I?" He gestured at my cot.

I scooted down to make room for him to sit beside me. The cot was small, and we were big, so our legs brushed though neither of us moved away.

"I am sorry if I was rough with you in the mines. It's best that the guards not see you associating with me. How are you feeling after your first day?"

"Fine. I'm no stranger to hard work."

"No, I didn't think so. But working here is harder work than most."

"It's draining, isn't it? Do you miss the sun?"

"Every day." Arun shifted slightly, tilting his head up as if he could still feel it on his face. "And the wind on my face as I soar through the sky, and the patter of rain on wooden decks, and the easy banter of free men." He smiled, but it felt sad in the way that remembering a loved one who had passed did, like an eternal ache somewhere deep inside. "But this isn't about me. I came to check on you."

I wanted to tell him that it was about him, but I wasn't sure that this was the time for the big reveal. "Well, thanks. I'm fine. How is Bertol?"

"Also fine," Arun said. "Recovering. He gets attacks sometimes, maybe due to the years he's spent down here. Some say that the dust turns our insides to coal over time. Another reason for us to wash it off at the end of the day—to delay our decay."

"How's your arm?"

He gave me a puzzled look.

"Where you took the lash."

"Oh." Arun looked surprised and held his arm out for inspection. "Not a mark."

"Wow." That was impressive. His close proximity and easy banter were strange to me. Usually men were afraid of me or pretended I didn't exist, but Arun Phina made me feel seen.

"It was good of you to talk to Xalph."

So he had been watching me. "I like him. He seems like a nice kid."

"He is. Especially considering he has Luthair blood in him."

I turned to look at Arun, leaning away. "I thought he was Haklang's son."

"Oh, he is." He didn't elaborate, and before I could ask more questions, he changed the subject. "So it's not every day we get a new body down here. Luthair reserves these depths for people who've really pissed him off. What did you do?"

I considered lying, and then I considered telling a half truth. But I felt like Arun Phina needed to know. I only had three days, after all. "I plotted with an elven woman named Tsarra Trisfina to free you."

"You— Tsarra—" He stood and someone from a nearby cot shushed him. He lowered his voice. "What?"

So, in a hushed voice, I told him everything about my meeting with Tsarra and my brother's refusal to help. About Tsarra's promise of passage out of Bruhier and safety in Lamruil. About Luthair's offers and finally, his threat to have my brother take Arun's place.

He was quiet for a time, taking in all the details. "Tsarra came to Barepost?"

I shrugged. "That's your takeaway?" If I was being honest, it irked me that he seemed to appreciate her small act of kindness over my own bravery. I wasn't in this to be the hero, but I wouldn't turn my nose up at a "thank you."

"No, I mean, it's just . . . You don't know her. She isn't the type. She must be truly desperate."

"It seemed she would do anything for her family. As would I."

Arun sat back down and rested his elbows on his knees. This time, where we touched, it felt like my skin was on fire, crackling between us with secrets. "Why are you here, then? What do you want, if freeing me means enslaving your brother?"

"I think that with your help, it won't come to that. We've wasted three years on Bruhier, and it's time to go home, all of the Svands. I took a chance coming here with the hopes that you're the one to help me do it."

He considered me again, this time looking more amused than baffled, and I felt hopeful for the first time since entering the mine. "Well, your gamble might just pay off. I have at my disposal the only method of travel from Barepost that doesn't require Governor Luthair's permission."

"Which is?"

"A ship."

I thought of the *Green Gem* at the wharf and the heavily monitored and patrolled marina. Luthair had complete control over the ships' comings and goings, signing every single departure notice. If we were discovered missing, he would stop all marine traffic, search every ship leaving the wharf. "You—"

"An airship."

"A what?"

"A *flying* ship."

I studied his face—the square jawline and long, straight nose, the perfectly arched brows over dark, bottomless eyes—waiting for the joke. But it never came. "There's no such thing." Then I remembered him telling me about missing the wind on his face as he soared through the air, and my conviction wavered.

"Oh, I assure you there are. Dozens dock at Lamruil, but

they stay above the veil, so they are out of reach of Bruhier's monsters."

There was a small noise at the entrance to the sleeping quarters, barely audible from where we sat, but Arun held a finger to his lips. A figure moved into the small square of light, paused, and then out again, footsteps fading down the corridor.

"The only problem," Arun said in an even quieter voice than before, "is that they're always watching."

It was true. After he returned to his own cot, I lay on mine for hours, waiting and listening. To the gentle snoring of other miners and to the footsteps of the guards patrolling the mine-shaft. Guards whose only job was to keep us inside, when all we wanted was a breath of fresh air and the wind on our faces.

CHAPTER 10

Bertol was back the next day. I was taken off of sorting duty and moved to extractions.

"What's this?" I asked when the guard handed me a pickax with a blade so dull it was practically round. I rubbed it with my finger to show him.

He wasn't concerned. "Your ax."

I was pretty sure he was smirking when he said it, as if he knew Luthair had my real ax and that if I'd had it, he would be dead by now. The shovel he gave me was about two feet too short for me, but I snatched it from him without complaint. Then, before I could leave and fall in line with my group, he added. "You have to fill four carts today before dinner."

"What?"

"Your quota," he said, holding up four fingers as if I would not be able to count that high otherwise. "Four carts. Per day. Which means you owe us two more for yesterday, four for today, and four more tomorrow before your sentence ends."

"Does anyone else—"

"Come on." A hand on my shoulder stopped me from arguing and I turned to see Arun Phina smiling at the guard.

"Four carts is nothing." He kept his hand on my shoulder until we were in the tunnel as if he thought I would turn around and demand answers from the guard otherwise. He probably wasn't wrong.

We made our way down the tunnel with careful steps. He helped me with the clips and the rope when I needed it but didn't say anything else.

Down in the mineshaft, Bertol and two other men from Arun's team worked our section of the seam with me, extracting and sorting in turns.

I moved to Bertol. "How are you feeling?"

The old man waved me off. "Right as rain." Then he looked up at me from the conveyor belt that was moving the rock in front of him. "When's the last time you saw rain?"

At first, I thought he was kidding, but then realized he'd probably been down here much longer than I could imagine. "Practically every day." The better question would be, when did I last appreciate the rain? I wouldn't have had an answer to that.

We worked tirelessly through the morning, but when Xalph came down to deliver lunch, we had only loaded one cart.

"Luthair's doing it to you on purpose." Xalph plopped down next to me.

I had already guessed as much, but it was nice to confirm it wasn't all in my head.

"The quota, anyway. The crap tools are because the guards don't like you."

"Gee, thanks." I grabbed a bag of lunch.

Xalph slapped my hand. "Not that one."

"What?"

"This one." He picked a larger bag out of the bottom of his basket and handed it to me. Something crinkled inside. Xalph looked over his shoulder. Satisfied that the guards weren't watching, he gestured for me to open it.

Inside was a folded piece of parchment, the creased lines so thin and worn that it was obvious the yellowed paper had been folded and unfolded countless times. I held the paper down low so no one would see it and studied the image drawn on it in charcoal. It took me only a few seconds to realize I was looking at a rough map of the mines.

I looked up at Xalph. "Is this—"

"A map? That I drew? Yes." He beamed. He pointed at a spot near the bottom of the page. "We're here. The original entryway has been blocked off, but there are still paths that might lead to exits on the ocean side of the cliff. I'll have to look at those tonight."

I followed his finger as he pointed out the edge of the mountain where it curved out into the ocean on the opposite side of the island from Barepost's wharf. "You shouldn't. It's dangerous." But a good idea. There wouldn't be anyone over there to catch us.

He smirked. "I'm not afraid."

"I didn't say you were."

He continued. "The ventilation shafts are too small. I haven't been able to fit through them for five years." His finger traced other lines, all of them ending at the top of the mountain.

I studied the map while I ate and Xalph passed out everyone else's lunches. The more I saw, the more hopeless it looked. There was no obvious way out except the main entrance, and there was no way Arun and I could just march out without being noticed.

"Can I keep this?" I asked Xalph when he came back by to collect trash.

He nodded. "Sure."

"Why are you doing this? Why are you helping us? Won't your dad be mad?"

"Da?" He cocked his head to the side, looking genuinely like he'd never considered it before. "I'm breaking him out too."

He left and I went back to work, hacking at the coal until my hands and sleeves were black with dust. The map, folded up in one of the pockets of my tool belt, felt like it weighed a ton. It tugged on me all afternoon. I didn't have long to figure out how to get out of here. Arun's airship was certainly the best option we'd ever had, and the only one that didn't require Luthair's permission. It occurred to me that I didn't necessarily even need Arun, not if I could find someone to pilot the airship. Harbin was my only connection to the sailing world, though, and he was gone. Who knew when he would return? But if I could get Arun out, and we could find the airship . . . Even my brother would have to see that this was the best plan we were ever likely to encounter. He'd done so much for Barepost. There was no way anyone would consider his life-debt unpaid.

But how could I do it? Could I rally the men in just one day? Inspire them to rebel against the guards? There were certainly plenty of men to do it, but I didn't know that they'd even want to revolt. They all seemed pretty resigned to their fates.

There were the ocean-side exits that Xalph suspected still existed. I wondered if they were accessible and, if they were, how Arun and I would ever get away. A distraction, maybe?

And I couldn't shake the idea of the ventilation shafts. Could I reach one via the outside and tunnel my way down into the mine? How long would it take me? And could I even reach the top of the mountain? I'd never gone higher than Barepost, never been above the veil.

We'd filled three carts when the bell rang for dinner. A guard, the same one from the first day who'd tried to beat Bertol, stopped at our small group as the others were filing out around us.

"I see you'll be here a little longer tonight." He knocked a boot against the next empty cart that had been wheeled into position in front of me.

Bertol and the other men shifted uncomfortably but didn't object.

I turned to them. "You all go on. This isn't your quota to meet."

"You think you can do it alone, then, D'ahvol?" The guard rubbed his thumb across the handle of the whip in his belt. "You think you are so much better than us humans?"

One of the other men raised his eyes to mine.

I realized shamefully that I didn't even know his name. "No. But why should they be punished because Governor Luthair doesn't like me?"

The guard sneered at me. "Does anyone like you?"

"I do." Arun entered my line of sight with a shovel over his shoulder, sweat glistening on his wide brow. He'd stayed away all day, probably lost in his own thoughts about his betrothed and his imminent escape. I was just glad he wasn't as stubborn as my brother, who would insist on serving the duration of his sentence, no matter if it meant dying below the mountain.

The guard was unfazed by his appearance though. "Anyone of any real importance, I meant."

Arun laughed like he hadn't just been insulted. Then he sobered. "I'm the team leader. I'll stay and finish the last cart with her."

"No—" I started.

"The rest should go to dinner."

The guard looked uncertain, and I realized that Arun meant the guard should go too.

Arun shrugged. "Where are we going to go? I've been here long enough to know there's no way out except back the way we came."

He had a plan, a way out. Why else would he be so adamant that everyone else leaves? I tried to look as innocent as possible, not something I had any practice at.

With a grunt, the guard nodded and turned to Bertol and the others who'd been watching quietly. "To the mess hall with you." He pointed a finger at Arun. "No funny business. The cart will be full when I come back for you or it will be lashings for the both of you."

Arun nodded. I wondered how common it was to receive lashings down here if it was the accepted form of punishment.

The group departed, the echoes of their footsteps fading slowly away.

I looked at Arun. "So?" I was ready to be done with this place. I'd spent all day hopelessly spinning my wheels and coming up with nothing. What I needed was a win, and I thought Arun might have it.

"So." He hefted his shovel in one hand and pickax in the other. "Get digging."

And to my surprise, that was exactly what he did.

CHAPTER 11

Arun's ax hit the seam of coal, burying itself deep in the crumbling wall. Arun tugged, breaking free a large chunk of black rock and tossing it behind him. Then he lifted the ax again.

"Wait," I said before he could swing. "Don't you have a plan?"

"A plan?" He looked back at me. "For what?"

I dropped my hands to my side. "I don't know. Escape, maybe? Isn't that why you wanted to get rid of the guard?"

His brow furrowed. "I just figured we would finish faster without you butting heads with him all night."

My gaze went to the cart, then back to the wall and the single rock that Arun had broken free. I really had to do this. I was going to leave this mine a failure and would have to face my brother and sister, and worst of all, have to admit they were right. There was no way to free Arun, at least not like this. The only thing left, the only thing I hadn't considered, was making a bargain with Luthair. Giving him one thing that he wanted that he never did have. Free Erik and Arun, and trap myself.

Was it worth it?

His eyes narrowed, and he bit his bottom lip as if he knew I was assessing his value. He was handsome and kind, and maybe more importantly, he was needed. Someone needed him to save their family, and I certainly understood that. Maybe by saving the Trisfina family, I could save my own too.

I picked up my ax. "Tell me about the ship." I drove the ax into the coal. My arms burned with fatigue, but I didn't mind the hard work. It was better than lying in the dark, driving myself mad with worry.

He smiled, returning to his work. "She's called the *Iron Duchess*. I won her off of another gentry elf in Lamruil when he challenged me to a duel."

A duel? The D'ahvol did not waste our time or our talent on foolish games, but I was intrigued just the same. "And if you had lost? What would he have won?"

"My estate."

"Your whole estate?"

He shrugged, chucking another rock into the cart. "I have no use for it."

I considered that. For all that I wanted to explore the world, it was always a comfort to know that Bor'sur and our family home would be waiting for my return. That I had somewhere to go when I was tired and weary, somewhere to call my own with my own people. And here Arun was, willing to give all of that up in a game between nobles. He'd also given up his freedom without a second thought while I'd been fighting to regain mine for three years. It seemed to maybe be a difference between us that wasn't worth arguing over, so I changed the subject.

"And how does she fly, your *Iron Duchess*?" A piece of coal broke off in my hand, staining my fingers, and I tossed it behind me into the cart.

Arun grinned at me. "Magic."

Of course. Magic. The D'ahvol could fight and survive in a hostile environment, but one thing we couldn't do was cast spells. We had no connection to the elements or to the ley lines that were said to run beneath the soils and waters of Iynia. The only advantage we had over humans other than our size and strength was that we were actually able to resist most magical influence. So not only could we not perform magic, we repelled it.

"Is it hidden by magic too? I haven't seen an airship hanging around Barepost."

"She's not in Barepost."

"Where is it, then?"

He pointed up.

I raised my eyes to the ceiling, which was mere inches above my head. "I left her on top of this very mountain under the guard of a few friends. Though the mission has taken longer than expected, I am confident they're still waiting for me."

"What makes you think they'll still be waiting for you?" I didn't have much experience with friends, but I didn't know any who would wait for anyone this long on this forsaken island.

"When I left them with my ship, they vowed to wait for my return if I could free their comrade from this very mine. And dragons are typically creatures of their word."

Dragons? Luthair had imprisoned a dragon in the mine? I could see the benefits. A large, strong creature like that could move a lot of rocks. But the fire? That seemed like a great risk for someone like Luthair. With the galestone and gasses and coal-dust, the mines were a dangerous enough place without a fire-breathing beast roaming their innards. I couldn't even imagine a whole group of them perched on top of this mountain, hidden from Barepost by the ever-present veil of clouds.

"All we have to do," Arun said, "is make it to the top."

"Have you ever climbed to the top?" I had, and it was a harrowing climb up the cliff face.

"No, but how hard can it be?" Arun shrugged.

I snorted. "It's hard."

The monsters of Bruhier didn't just exist on ground level. So not only did we have to climb a sheer mountainside, we had to do it while fighting off monsters. But Arun Phina didn't seem like the type that could be told anything. He would just have to see the truth for himself—if I could figure out a way to get him out of here, which was a big if, then he'd have to get himself up to the plateau. Bruish elves were said to be fierce fighters. I hoped it was true.

The cart was half-full and we fell into an easy silence as we worked, both of us lost in our own thoughts. The piece of the seam where I was working was becoming narrower, the rocks breaking off in larger, easier chunks.

It had to be nearing the middle of the night when I drove my ax into the rock one more time with enough force that it buried itself to the handle. Bracing my foot against the wall, I gave the ax-handle a tug, but it was stuck. Arun looked over, tossed his own ax to the ground, and held his hand out for mine. While I didn't like the idea of being rescued by a man, he'd been doing this type of work longer than I had, so I relinquished the ax. The handle stuck out of the rock like a lever, almost like if I pulled it the right way, it would open a door to a room beyond.

Arun gave the ax a tug. "This is very strange. Like it's caught on something on the other side."

More rock, I thought dubiously. Bruhier had never come through for me before. I didn't expect it to now. That was why, when he gave another mighty pull on the handle and it broke free, ripping away a huge chunk of rock, I didn't believe what was right before my eyes.

A tunnel.

Or at least, a hole.

Arun thought the same thing. He reached a hand inside and it disappeared up to his shoulder. Then he looked back at me, eyes wide with wonder as if I'd had something to do with this discovery. As if I were magic.

He began clawing at the rock and it crumbled away, sheets of black coal coating the ground at his feet. I joined him until the hole was large enough for someone to duck through, a tiny doorway to another world. Arun peered inside.

"What is it?" I asked.

"Our way out," he said, and with that, he stepped through and disappeared.

CHAPTER 12

I watched the black doorway and, for a brief moment, wondered if he would ever come back.

Then his smiling face reappeared. "You won't believe this."

"Believe what?" a voice came from behind.

My heart in my throat, I whipped around, ready to use my blunt ax to bludgeon someone to death. But then Xalph limped into view, peering behind me with his good eye. Thankfully, he was alone.

"Onen save me," I gasped, a hand to my chest.

"Not Onen," Arun said, with a grin. "Me."

I tucked my pickax into one of my belt loops. "I'm the one who found it."

He smiled smugly anyway.

"Found what?" Xalph stepped carefully over the discarded rock. "I didn't see you guys at dinner. I thought something—" He stopped talking when the hole came into view. "What is that?"

"A tunnel," Arun said.

"A tunnel to where?" Xalph squinted into the dark.

I pulled the folded map from my back pocket and smoothed it out against a nearby wall.

Xalph and I both peered at it.

"Here." Xalph put his finger to the spot where we were supposedly standing. "There shouldn't be anything there."

"Well, I'm standing in it, so I'd say it doesn't care if you think it should be here or not." Arun cheerfully leaned his arms against the stone around the doorway.

Xalph, fearless Xalph, bit his lip. "Bruhier can be tricky." He couldn't have been older than ten, but he sounded much older.

"He's right." I turned to Arun and let Xalph take the map.

He studied it intently, as if this secret passage would just appear out of sheer willpower. "Who knows why that tunnel is there . . . Or what's living inside of it."

"Why don't we find out?" Arun sounded exactly like someone who had never come face to face with a Bruhier monster. He held out a hand. "Xalph, you have a light?"

Absently, his eyes still on his hand-drawn map, Xalph unbuckled the small oil lamp he carried on his belt and handed it to Arun.

"What if the guards come back for us?" I wasn't worried about myself, but more worried about what would happen to him if he were discovered here and we weren't.

He glanced up, realizing we were watching him. "You guys go. I'll keep watch and distract anyone who comes this way if I have to. Just don't be gone too long."

I wanted to ask what would happen to him if we didn't come back at all but bit my tongue. It wasn't my problem. I was here to get Arun out, that was all. Arun stepped aside, and I ducked into our ragged doorway. It smelled strange, of damp soil and decay instead of cold rock and sweaty bodies. The lamp flared to life, and Arun held it up, illuminating a large, round tunnel that tapered into darkness. Something on the rock wall caught my attention—three long, deep grooves carved into the dirt and stone.

I walked over and ran my fingers along them, knowing in an instant what had made this tunnel. "A gloomling."

But Arun was right behind me. The lamp cast my shadow down the length of the tunnel. "A what?"

"A gloomling dug this tunnel," I repeated, remembering the massive, three-fingered claw Erik had dragged from the mine. "A cave monster."

Arun held the lamp up higher and searched the darkness. "Is it still here, do you think?"

"No. I don't think." The truth was, I could only hope that the gloomling who had dug this tunnel was the same one Erik had hunted and killed and that he hadn't left any family members behind. But then again, like Xalph said, Bruhier could be tricky. I didn't know how common gloomlings were or even if they were the worst thing we could encounter.

We followed the tunnel, Arun holding the light high for us to see by. I kept expecting the tunnel to end, for us to run up against an impenetrable wall that would effectively put an end to our escape plan, but it never did. It went on and on in a straight line, like a road to the center of the world. One good thing was that I did not see any evidence of a live gloomling— no fresh tracks or food scraps or scat.

We'd walked for at least ten minutes when Arun paused and raised the lamp even higher, his hand hitting the rock ceiling. He squinted into the darkness, then dropped his hand and twisted the knob on the lamp to extinguish it.

"What—" I started, but paused. Instead of being plunged into darkness, there was a faint glow lighting the path ahead of us. "What is it?"

"Have you heard of yooperlite?" He moved forward again.

I shook my head, wary of yet another surprise from this blasted island. "No."

"It's a glowing rock, a natural source of light. I've only ever seen it around Lamruil, but—"

He didn't get to finish. One minute he was in front of me, and the next he was gone. I took a step before I could stop myself and suddenly, I was falling, sliding along the rock, my feet and hands scrambling for something to grab. The tunnel, which had been flat and straight, had become a ramp, declining at a sharp angle. Arun was just in front of me. I felt my feet brush his shoulders. I tried to brace my arms or my legs against the tunnel walls, but they were too slick, too round, too far apart. The worst part was not the falling, but the not knowing what was waiting for us at the end, or if we would survive it.

"Frida!" Arun's hand went around my ankle, and I felt myself falling faster. I didn't like the panic in his voice and wondered what he could see that I couldn't. I thought of the gloomling and fumbled in my belt for the pickax. If that monster had made it up here, so could I—I just needed a claw.

I freed the ax from its holster and dragged it along the ground. It slowed us a little but didn't find purchase. My arms were raw and my legs ached.

"Frida!" Arun yelled again, his voice desperate.

I wanted to tell him to stop. To stop saying my name like I could do something. To stop relying on me. To save himself. But I couldn't find the breath to make a sound, not even a scream.

We were slowing down, and the tunnel was growing brighter. I could see Arun's hand around my ankle, see the blood on my palm, and see the brown dirt and grey rock of the walls around us. And I could see the end of our tunnel and beyond it, an enormous cavern lit yellow by what I could only assume was Arun's yooperlite.

I dug in my ax, twisting around and using both hands. Dirt kicked up into my face, and I felt the warmth of blood sliding down my chin. There was a hard jerk and Arun was airborne, his hand still around my ankle, taking me with him. I held my breath and beseeched the gods to spare me. I had so much more to do, so much more to see, that it couldn't end like this, broken on a cavern floor. I was meant to die beneath the stars, not here, in the dark underground.

The ax caught.

Still holding onto the ax handle, I jerked to a stop, my body slamming against the cavern wall. Arun still had my ankle, and he was dangling beneath me, and below him, there was nothing but a bottomless pit of light. I thought this might be the entrance to Ash'gar if there was one in this mortal world.

"Don't let go."

Arun didn't respond. Instead, I felt another hand wrap around my other ankle. I ground my teeth, straining not to lose my grip. I would not—could not—let go. He hoisted himself up the length of my body until he finally reached the lip of the ledge and hauled himself up. Then he turned back to me, grabbed my wrists, and pulled me over. I collapsed onto the ground beside him and closed my eyes.

"Thank Onen," he said, his voice shaky and quiet.

I looked over at him. "Not Onen," I echoed his earlier statement. "Me."

He smiled weakly. "Thank you."

We were both exhausted but didn't have the time to waste feeling sorry for ourselves. We had to figure out a way to get back to the mine before Xalph got caught. I pushed myself up beside him and brushed my hands on my dirty tunic. Arun took one of my hands in his and examined the scraped, bleeding palm. Then he ripped a small swath of cloth from the bottom of his linen shirt and wrapped it around the worse of the cuts, tying it off in a tight knot.

"That should hold until we can get you washed up." He wasn't looking much better himself. His hair was a tangled mess and his face was streaked with dirt and dust. His pants were ripped, too, with a long, jagged tear down the side.

I thanked him and stood, taking in our surroundings. We stood on a ledge only a couple of feet wide and several hundred feet above the ground. The cavern was unfathomably large, as large as the mountain itself, it felt like, and was crisscrossed by natural stone bridges. Some were impassable, crumbling and narrow, but others looked sturdy enough to hold us and help us maneuver through the cavern.

"Shall we?" Arun took a few tentative steps along the ledge. One of the bridges was a few feet below us to our right. I followed him as we dropped onto it. "There's a tunnel up there that might take us back." He pointed to an opening overhead. "But I want to take a look around first."

We walked, crossing bridges and exploring dark tunnels full of minerals and more yooperlite. In some places, the walls glistened with gold. I wondered if I could use my knowledge of this place to bargain with Luthair, or if he already knew and just hadn't decided to expand the mine yet. I just couldn't imagine him willingly leaving so many resources untapped, though. As we walked, Arun showed me how yooperlite worked, how the warmer it was, the brighter it glowed. He told me about how they strung it in the trees and danced all night at their revels by its eerie, yellow glow. He told me more about his airship and how it felt to fly, and I told him about the Western March, putting voice to memories I hadn't spoken about in years. I told him about my father and our house at the tip of the world, about learning to fight with Erik and Estrid, about boarding a ship for the first time and sailing away from the only place I'd ever known.

We were in a dark, damp tunnel, moving forward by the light of a yooperlite stone Arun held in his hand, when he stopped suddenly, putting a finger to his lips.

"In here," he whispered, pulling me into an alcove in the wall.

"What is it?"

He leaned forward to peer out of our hiding place, then

looked back at me, pointing to his eyes and then out into the tunnel, telling me to see for myself. That was when I heard it, the scrape of feet on rock, the swish of a tail sweeping along the floor, the shallow breaths of a creature hunting something.

My hand on the ax, I leaned out.

The creature was no bigger than a dog but looked more like a dock rat than a four-legged pet. Its snake-like body was low to the ground and its feet ended in long, sharp claws that could have been good for digging or tearing apart its prey. Two large flat teeth protruded from the front of its snout, but its eyes were tiny black orbs, barely visible. It was obviously a creature who lived in the dark.

I pushed myself back against the wall beside Arun and moved to draw the ax, but Arun stilled me with a hand on mine and a shake of his head. I wanted to argue. I'd killed every monster I'd ever come across in Bruhier. It was just what I did, what was expected of me. But Arun was adamant, shoving my hand away.

There was no time to argue, though. The monster was only a few feet away, its snout in the air. I wondered if it could smell the blood on my hand, maybe the sweat on my brow. I imagined its claws ripping into me, its teeth on my neck. It turned to me, fixing me with its beady black eyes, and I held my breath as it stretched its neck out, its teeth coming within inches of my face.

Every part of me screamed to strike, but I remembered Arun's hand on mine. I slid my eyes over to Arun and he was watching the creature with a strange mix of awe and respect on his face. His right hand slipped into my left and squeezed in what I hoped was reassurance. The creature sniffed at us, then made a huffing sound as if he didn't like what he smelled, and trotted away, back toward the cavern in the direction we'd come.

I exhaled heavily and relaxed back against the wall. "What was it?"

"A cave dragon, I think. I've never seen one before, but I've heard about them."

"How did you know it wouldn't kill us?" I kept my voice low, resisting the urge to yell at him for his foolishness.

Arun cocked his head at me. "I didn't. But you can't go around killing everything that has claws, now, can you?"

Before I could beg to differ, he'd pushed himself out of our alcove and turned away from the cavern. I followed, glancing over my shoulder for any signs of the monster, seeing none. "Shouldn't we go back?"

"Just a little farther."

We followed the tunnel, only a few yards before coming to its end. The rock wall looked immovable and solid.

"It had to have come from somewhere," Arun muttered as if to himself.

I looked at the walls on either side of us, at the floor, solid beneath our feet, and then lifted my eyes to the ceiling. There it was, the small opening, and beyond it, the black sky, nearly blending with the rock interior of the mountain. I tapped Arun on the shoulder and pointed.

He went still the moment his eyes found the opening and the sky beyond.

CHAPTER 13

Arun dragged me back down the tunnel and into the yooperlite cavern without saying a word, ignoring my protests.

"Why are we going back?" I asked when he let go of me to cross a narrow stone bridge.

"I can't let Xalph take the fall for us." But he was acting strangely. If it was just that he wanted to keep Xalph safe, I didn't think he'd have this excited, buzzing energy around him.

"You can't tell anybody, Arun."

"I won't." But he didn't look back at me, and that was how I knew he was lying.

We found our way through the maze of tunnels back to the one that would deliver us to the mineshaft without incident, though I kept my eyes open for any gloomling or cave dragon that might dare to cross our path. The mineshaft was quiet, and Arun stepped aside to let me through first. I was nearly there, only one leg still in the tunnel, when I raised my head and saw who greeted us.

Xalph was there, but so was his father.

Haklang and Xalph stood a few yards from the doorway,

Xalph wide-eyed and anxious while his father was grim-faced and stern.

Arun pushed me out of the way as he shoved himself through the doorway, but he also froze when he saw Haklang.

"I can—"

Haklang held up a hand. His other hand was gripping his son's shoulder so hard that his fingertips were white. Xalph didn't seem to notice. "I won't say anything. I won't even stop you, but on one condition."

Why wasn't I surprised? I'd found myself entering into so many bargains lately that I was going to lose track. I was relieved, though, glad that we had something to bargain with and that he wasn't just going to turn us over to Luthair. If he did, Erik would never see the light of day again.

"What's that?" Arun asked.

"You take Xalph with you when you leave."

"When we leave?" I pretended not to know what he meant.

He slipped into Ahvoli. "Do you think I don't know what's on the other side of that wall? What lies deep in the mountain? Or why you are here, even?"

I didn't know why I bothered to keep anything a secret when everyone seemed to know what was going on. "Then why did you let this happen?"

Arun was watching us blankly.

"Because you might be Xalph's only chance to get out of the mine," he said in Iynian so that Arun would understand. "Years ago, when I first arrived in Bruhier, I fell in love with Albree Luthair."

I knew the name but just in passing. Albree Luthair was Stephan's older sister and Aysche's mother. As I understood it, she'd died giving birth to a baby boy, Aysche's younger brother, and the baby had died also.

I studied Xalph's face and realized that maybe not all of that story was true. Albree had had an affair with Haklang, and the child had killed her. His punishment? Life in the mines, for both the father and the illegitimate child. Suddenly, Xalph's life in the dark, while certainly not justified, made sense, especially knowing Luthair.

Haklang nodded, seeming to know that I understood. "As long as he lives here, he will live under the shadow of the Luthair family. I don't care about me, but I want better for my son. Our son." He looked down at Xalph, who hadn't looked away from Arun and me, and I knew he was trying to figure out how angry we would be with him. "Even if it means facing Luthair's wrath. I have been too afraid for too long."

I didn't want to take Xalph. I didn't want to saddle myself with another debt, another responsibility. Especially a child who was crippled and half-blind. But the last thing he said, about being afraid, tugged at something inside of me. I'd also been afraid, and Erik and Estrid. Afraid of losing, afraid of leaving. I saw my future in Haklang's face if I didn't leave.

I couldn't pledge myself to Luthair and then beg someone, decades later, to take my children away from here, to give them the life I hadn't been able to. Haklang had chosen this life, but Xalph hadn't. "Fine. We'll take him if we go."

"When we go," Arun corrected me, though he still couldn't look me in the eye.

Haklang helped us to fill the last cart and hide the hole we'd made in the wall behind a stack of broken-down carts and discarded tools. Then he escorted us back to the depot where we ate cold slop in silence before he deposited us in our sleeping quarters.

Sequestered in my little corner, I used a wash basin filled with cold water to clean myself the best I could while trying not to make any noise that would wake the sleeping men, although some of their snoring was loud enough to wake the dead. I unwrapped my hand, draping the makeshift bandage on the edge of the wash basin, and dabbed at the gash there. It was still open and bleeding. I would probably need stitches, though I hated to think about how it might affect my ability to hold an ax. I also rolled my pants to the knee and washed the dirt from my legs and arms, longing all the while for the private room in the hot springs.

I'd just stripped down to my linen undershirt when I saw a dark figure moving through the room, headed toward me.

"Good," Arun whispered. "You're still awake." He was in his undershirt and wearing clean britches, his feet bare and his hair loose and damp. When it was down like that, it covered his ears and made it easy to forget that he wasn't human, though the sharp beauty of his face did lend itself to his elven heritage.

I expected him to want to talk about what we'd found and what had happened today, but instead, I saw him reach over to Bertol and shake the old man awake, then several others, all before I could stop him.

Before I knew it, the entirety of Group A was gathered around my bunk in their nightclothes, eyes half-closed with sleep.

"Frida and I found something tonight," Arun said in a low voice. "A tunnel. A way out."

"A way out?" Bertol perked up.

Arun put a hand on Bertol's shoulder. "A way out for all of us. As many as want to go."

I bit my tongue to stop myself from interjecting. What was he talking about? We were already saddled with Xalph, and now he was offering to get everyone else out too? Bertol, with his bad heart. Owin, with his one good hand. While they talked in low, excited whispers about the tunnel we'd found, all I could think about was how we were doomed. He was an idiot, and we were doomed.

"I can't wait for you to see it," Arun said. "It's just full of yooperlite."

"Yooperlite." Bertol smiled around at the others. "I've only ever heard of it."

"Arun," I interrupted, tugging on his sleeve. "Can I have a word?" I couldn't keep quiet, couldn't bite my tongue, not if I wanted to succeed.

He nodded, and we took a couple steps away, stopping in front of an empty cot nearby. He leaned over so that his ear was close to my ear, and I hated how his nearness made my heart race.

I felt like I was sliding down a tunnel again, not sure what was waiting for me at the end. I cleared my throat with the hopes that it would also clear my head. "This wasn't the bargain I made with Tsarra," I said finally.

He drew back a little and looked at me, eyebrows knit together, drawing three lines in the middle of his brow.

"I promised to get you out, and in exchange, you would get me and my siblings out of Barepost."

"That's still the plan," Arun confirmed.

"The more people involved, the less likely you are to succeed. I'm going to have to carry Xalph up the mountain as it is. How are you going to get Bertol up? And Owin? He can get by with one hand in the sorting line, but not climbing a cliff face."

Arun, who had been so warm and excited, closed himself off, pulling away from me. "I won't leave them here. Do you know why Bertol is here?"

"That's not—"

"Because he stood up to a guard who was beating a little boy. Does he deserve to be down here with murderers and thieves? And Owin? He lost his hand in the same mining accident that crippled Xalph. If he hadn't been there, the boy would have been crushed to death. Do you just want to leave them here to serve a life sentence?"

I sighed. "We can't always do the right thing. Sometimes we just have to do the best thing. The best thing for us."

He lifted his head indignantly, looking like the gentry elf he was. "Someone has to make things right, and I'm not afraid for it to be me."

I shook my head. There was no arguing with him. I now knew what Tsarra meant, then, about him dying for a cause, how it hadn't been a figure of speech but an actual description of his character. He would fight for what was morally right, no matter the cost—to himself or to others. It was a noble idea, but in practice, putting yourself out there to die for any cause—be it to free a dragon, to help an elven family, or to rescue an entire group of prisoners—seemed foolish. *Was* foolish. Every now and then, people had to look out for themselves, to survive. People like me and Erik and Estrid who needed off of this island.

This wasn't the way to do it. This was the way to get us all captured or killed. And if Luthair discovered my hand in the plot, Erik would be in the mines for the rest of his life.

I left Arun to make his plans, lying down in my cot and turning my back to the group while I tried to decide what to do. Because I had something else to bargain with now. Information.

Maybe I wouldn't have to trade my hand in marriage for my siblings' freedom. Maybe I could buy all our freedom with information about the cave system and Arun's planned escape. I just had to find a way to get the information to Luthair before Arun did something we would all regret in the end.

CHAPTER 14

Fu Shen, the god of luck, was on my side when, at breakfast the next morning, a cart rumbled up to the depot. None other than Governor Luthair himself stepped out, brushing imaginary dust off of his deep-red cloak. At the other end of the table, Arun held court with Group A, discussing their plans for escape in hushed tones. Plans that I knew didn't matter. They would never make it out. Xalph was hovering nearby, looking both excited but uncertain. The group fell silent as they noticed our visitor.

It was Haklang who greeted him, just as he'd been the one to greet me. He crossed the room with long strides, cutting his eyes first at Arun, then at me, then stared resolutely ahead. "Governor. It's been too long. What a nice surprise."

A surprise? So, the visit was unplanned. Had someone betrayed Arun already? Had a guard seen us? Or perhaps Haklang was going back on his word, striking some other bargain with Luthair.

But when Luthair's eyes found me in the crowd of diners, I knew that none of that was true. I knew that he had come for me. It was my last day, after all. If I was still here, then he knew that any escape attempt would happen today. It was as if he'd been drawn to the smell of my doubt, of my weakness. It made me sick.

He and Haklang conferred briefly, and I could just imagine the conversation. Small talk about quotas and shipping costs and labor needs. The dining room was still quiet when Haklang returned and rang the dismissal bell.

I stood and joined my group.

Arun looked at me, then away, as if I no longer existed. Maybe to him, I didn't. I wasn't some lost cause or damsel in distress, after all. I could—and would—save myself.

A hand clapped down on my shoulder. "You're to stay," Haklang said in quiet Ahvoli. "The governor wishes to speak to you. Please . . ." He trailed off, looking away from me.

I followed his gaze to where Xalph was clearing plates from the dining tables and knew what he was asking me, knew what he couldn't say. Knew what I couldn't promise.

Arun saw us, and though he didn't understand, I thought he knew what was happening. He opened his mouth as if to speak. My heart stuttered, and I hated myself for it.

My own words got stuck in my throat. I should have told him that I was sorry. I should have told him that we could have saved each other, that we still could.

But neither of us spoke, both of us waiting on the other. Then he snapped his mouth shut and turned away, taking whatever sentiment or request or farewell into the mineshaft with him. I didn't call after him even though I desperately wanted to know, desperately wanted to speak my own apology.

The last of the miners disappeared down the tunnel after Arun. Even Haklang made himself scarce.

I felt Luthair's presence behind me, smelled the cloying floral scent of his perfume before I turned to face him. He stood close, his hands tucked in his cloak pockets, that small, self-assured smile on his face. He would have me believe he knew everything. I had to be careful about what I said or I would lose any bargaining power I had.

"Please," Luthair said, gesturing to the nearest chair as if we were in some grand dining hall. "Have a seat."

I obliged, only because I didn't think taunting him would get me anywhere, not when I needed him to be at least mildly agreeable. He seemed pleased as he took the seat across from me.

"Interesting to see how the mines have changed you in so few days," he said.

I scowled but bit my tongue. This was my chance to have him listen, to really try to free all of us—Erik, Estrid, and me—from his service. If I didn't, if I couldn't make him listen, if he wouldn't strike a deal, if I didn't betray Arun Phina, then what? Then it would be Erik in these mines, Estrid and I working for Luthair every day in the hopes of freeing him. Or it would be me, married to Stephan Luthair, sharing his home and his bed. It would be a lifetime squandered on this blasted island. One compromise of my honor, one elf sacrificed—it was worth it for our freedom.

But a small, nagging part inside of me told me that Erik wouldn't approve. A part of me that I tried to shove deep down inside.

"When I was a boy," he said, surprising me, "my father brought me across the sea from Center City to Bruhier in search of wealth. Do you know what he found?"

I could guess.

"A lawless country where monsters ruled, elves hid high on their plateaus, and humans fought each other for scraps of gold. I spent years in fear, never knowing if the next day would be the day that he or I would die."

I tried to imagine him as a young boy, as a child with a father and frivolous dreams and nightmares that kept him awake and failed.

To me, Luthair had always been the governor, a cruel and ruthless man. Then I compared it to my own childhood, to the love and safety and support that my father and siblings had given me. We had not had much, but I had at least known that they would keep me safe, no matter what. Even here, where monsters roamed, I felt safe fighting beside Erik and Estrid.

"When I was sixteen, my father was captured and sent to work the rest of his life in the mines. He wasn't a criminal or a miner. Just a man who had the bad luck to run into a band of slavers when he was alone at night. What do you think I did? Do you think I ran into the mines to rescue him? To save one person? To likely get myself trapped there with him?"

No, I didn't think that Luthair would do that. Not this cold, calculating man sitting in front of me. But maybe I would. In fact, I knew I would. I would sacrifice my life for someone I loved without hesitation. Without a second thought.

He didn't wait for me to answer, wasn't even looking at me as he spoke. He was somewhere else, someone else. "No. I left Barepost. I returned to Center City. I trained and worked and raised an army. And then, only when I was ready to make a real difference, did I return and march on Barepost. Years had gone by and my father was long dead, but did that mean it was all in vain? I learned from my father's mistakes. In his memory, I took the lawless town and made it into a thriving community. You think I am a monster, but really, I am just a man, someone's son and brother and, maybe someday, father, trying to make a difference in this world, doing the best that I can with what I have been given."

"What about the dragon?"

He'd been drumming his fingers on the table and now stilled, focusing on my face. "The dragon?"

"The dragon that you'd unlawfully sentenced to life in the mines. The one that Arun Phina came to free."

Luthair nodded. "That dragon and his friends destroyed one

of my ships, the *Flying Fox*, when it was returning to Barepost with food and livestock. An entire crew, an entire ship, lost. Dozens of men, a shipment worth its weight in gold. All for sport. He was the only one we caught. I made the bargain with Arun because he offered and because the creature was horribly stupid. He would have blown us all up if he'd stayed. Arun did me a favor. And now, he's one of the best I have."

"But he doesn't belong here."

"No one does," Luthair conceded with a shrug.

Silence hung between us, thick and uncomfortable. I didn't like this—seeing Luthair as a person rather than a monster.

"So," he said finally, "will you not be freeing him, then? Should I let you out early on good behavior?"

I thought about Arun and Haklang and Bertol, and about what Luthair said, about making a difference. About not saving just his father but saving the whole town. I knew one thing for certain, though. I couldn't save anyone from down here. "You win." The words tasted bitter on my tongue. "Erik's life is not mine to risk. I'm just here to serve out my sentence like a good citizen of Barepost."

Xalph was behind Luthair, wiping down a table.

I met his eye, and even though I couldn't say anything to him, I hoped that he would understand. That I wasn't ratting on him or Arun or Haklang. I was going to help them, damn my bleeding heart. Arun was determined to do this, and maybe I could be the one to make a difference, the key to his success. And if it got me and my siblings off the island in the meantime, well, that would be an added bonus.

My gaze dropped back to Luthair, who I was sure hadn't even noticed Xalph behind him. Did he even know his own nephew by sight?

"Excellent." Luthair stood. "Wonderful news. As governor of this wonderful town, I hereby declare your time served. Let's go." He held a smooth hand out to me.

I looked at it, then over at Xalph, and back to Luthair. "Now? Shouldn't I finish out my quota?"

"No need. I'll leave a message for Haklang."

I ignored his outstretched hand and stood. "So I'm free to go? I'll be home by tonight?" When I spoke, I raised my voice so Xalph would hear. I could only hope he was as smart as I thought he was. I needed him to tell Arun to delay their escape until tonight. To give me time to get up the mountain and find the opening from the other side.

"Sooner, if you hurry."

We walked to the waiting cart, him pushing me with a hand at the small of my back. I boarded the cart first and glanced back at Xalph, who stood watching us in the center of the room, the rag all but forgotten in his hand.

I widened my eyes at him, and it spurred him into action.

He tossed the rag to the side and hurried down the mine-shaft as quickly as he could with his awkward gait, not even glancing back to say goodbye.

It didn't matter, I told myself. I would see him soon anyway. On the other side.

CHAPTER 15

The ride back up the tracks was much slower than its descent had been, and Luthair was squeezed into the cart much too close to me for comfort. We passed dozens of empty and abandoned mineshafts and one cave-in. The entrance was barricaded with a pile of blocks, marked unsafe by two rotten wooden boards nailed across it. It made me think of Xalph and his life underground, and how truly lucky I was to be leaving.

We were the only ones in the entryway at this time of day. Everyone else was already at work. It felt lazy and slothful, but I reminded myself that this was not my job, digging up piles of rocks. I had something else to do.

But when we exited the mine and made our careful way down the hill, Luthair directed me to his house on the ridge instead of letting me go to Barepost.

"We still have some things to discuss," he said.

"It can't wait until I've cleaned up?" I hesitated at the fork in the path.

Luthair smiled. "If you want to clean up, I have the perfect place for it."

I hesitated. I needed to go to Erik and Estrid. I needed to get them up the mountain and find the entry to the tunnel where Arun would be bringing the miners. Was it worth angering Luthair to insist that I leave now? Would it be suspicious? Would he instead keep me trapped somewhere else? My hand itched for a weapon—killing him now wouldn't solve much, but it would at least solve this. Then I remembered that he had my ax and my sword, and I nodded once.

The house on the ridge was no less resplendent in daylight. The veil was thick, the sun overhead a yellow splotch against the white clouds. Still, it reflected off of the glass windows, the dull light blinding in its reflection. I followed Luthair past his sentries and into the massive front doors. Once in the foyer, instead of going up the stairs to the sleeping quarters, we turned left, going down a stone-walled hallway. We passed a kitchen twice as large as the one in the pub. It was quiet. The pots and pans were empty.

Luthair ushered me past and then opened a door on the right. A narrow stone staircase led down into a dark hallway. He lit a lantern on the wall and led me down. It felt like we were going back into the mine, and I wondered if this was some mean trick that I hadn't seen coming. But then the air became thick with steam, and the hallway opened up onto a large bathroom. Instead of stone, the walls were lined with wooden planks. In the middle, a claw-foot, porcelain tub was already filled with steaming water, and the mirror hanging over a wash basin was clouded with fog.

"For your bathing pleasure." He swept his hand in a grand gesture.

Well, it sure did beat a wash basin and a dirty cloth, but I would have taken the hot springs over Luthair's company any day.

I looked over at him. "Are you just going to stand there or are you going to let me get cleaned up?"

He crossed his arms over his chest and twisted his lips into a smile. It looked painful on his face. "I'm not stopping you."

Onen help me, I was going to kill him with my bare hands. I took a deep breath, then put a hand on the door. "Out."

For a moment, I thought he'd argue. "Fine. We'll continue our discussion over lunch."

Lunch, another delay. I slammed the door behind him and flipped the iron latch to keep him out. Even still, when I stripped out of my clothes and lowered myself into the water, I felt eyes on me. Just being under his roof made me uneasy. And it was made worse by my suspicions about why I was there. Luthair was showing off for me. Letting me know that this could all be mine for the low, low price of . . . the rest of my life.

The hot water relaxed my sore muscles just as the hot springs had done. Thinking of the springs made me think of Arun and our encounter there, and how the chills I got when I was near him were entirely different than the ones that crept up my spine when Luthair's leg had pressed against mine in the cart.

I tried to scrub the feeling away, turning my skin a rosy pink in the process. I had never been overly concerned with men. As a young girl in the Western March, I'd been too busy tagging along behind Erik and Estrid to really have much time for boys my age. I'd kissed a couple of them, though, and I'd let Hauk, the miller's son, go further than that just one time in his father's mill house, but my experience with physical attraction was limited, and with love, even more so. Not that I thought I loved Arun, though, for the first time, I wondered if I might actually want to love someone. To be with someone who gave me the good kind of chills.

And if I gave myself to Luthair, if I bound myself to him by marriage, it would be my own kind of life-debt. The kind that could never be broken. I would never have the chance to love or live. But what else was there, if I didn't get off the island with Arun tonight? It would be the only option left.

I finished bathing and wrapped myself in the softest towel I'd ever put against my skin, feeling terribly unworthy of its finery. Then I stood in front of the mirror and wiped it clean with my hand, trying to recognize the girl in front of me. She was tall and gaunt, with dark circles beneath grey eyes. Three days in the dark and three years under the veil had turned my skin an almost translucent white. My hair, usually kept short, had gotten too long, brushing the backs of my shoulders, spilling drops of cool water down my bare arms and back.

There was a knock on the door, but before I could snarl at Luthair to leave me in peace for another few minutes, a rough female voice demanded entry. I opened the door to find Missus, who greeted me with narrowed eyes and an unfriendly grunt, a bundle of clothes in her hands. I took them eagerly—linen trousers and a long tunic, and my own woolen cloak, leather jerkin, and worn, calf-skin boots. The only items missing were my weapons, but I would be sure to get those from Luthair before I left. Missus pulled my wet hair out of my face with a short, tight braid.

"What is this?" She tapped the star beside my eye and looked up at me in the mirror.

I put my own hand to the mark. "A blessing from my ancestors."

She squinted at me, then let her finger linger a moment longer beside my eye, her touch gentle.

I thought she might be about to say something. Then she shook her head and stepped away, giving me room to stand. "What is this?" This time, she was pointing at my hand.

I'd forgotten about the wound there, and its dull ache. After poking at it for a few seconds, she sat me back down without a word and pulled a bone needle and some sort of thick black thread from a drawer. She was not particularly gentle as she stitched the cut back together, but it wasn't the worst I'd ever experienced. When she was through, she rubbed some sort of ointment on it that took the sting of pain away and then wrapped it in a clean linen bandage.

She escorted me back up the stone hallway, past the kitchens, through the foyer, and into a large dining room. The entire eastern wall was made of glass and gave the dizzying sensation that we were stepping out onto the very ledge of the cliff itself. Barepost was a mere speck below us. What seemed like the whole of Bruhier stretched out as far as I could see. Mountains ringed with clouds towered over thick jungle below, canopies of rich green that hid horrors beyond my wildest imagination. And beyond even that, the blue-grey ocean sparkled in the midday sun.

Taken as I was by the view, it took me too long to notice Luthair sitting at the head of the large mahogany table set for two.

"Magnificent, isn't it, seen from up here?" He looked out over the landscape, acting as if he owned the entire world.

I heard what he didn't say—this view could be mine every day if I agreed to his terms. But I had other cards to play now. And besides, it was easy to look at things from a distance and call them beautiful. It was up close when a thing's true nature was revealed.

Instead of rising to his bait, I dropped my eyes to the table, sneering at him.

Missus grunted, in what I assumed was disapproval at my manners, and excused herself, leaving me alone with him.

"Please." He gestured to the chair. "Sit."

I did, sitting in the chair beside him, my back to the window. Lunch was already on the table—sliced mutton, roasted greens, and some type of grain. We served ourselves in silence, and I was glad for it. The less talking he did, the better, especially when the meat was tender enough that it fell off the bone. I didn't need him ruining the last good meal I was likely to have for a while.

After a few bites, though, he spoke up. "I'm surprised that you didn't follow through with your plan to save the elf."

I swallowed. "Why is that?"

"Well, he's handsome and wealthy, but I didn't think that would move you." Luthair leaned back in his chair, his eyes gleaming. "But he has a good heart. I thought that in itself would compel you. But I see you weren't swayed. Perhaps you and I are more alike than I originally thought."

I nearly choked at the idea.

"And there's the fact that my guards haven't been able to find your brother since you were imprisoned."

I dared not lift my eyes to his. I'd told my brother to steer clear of the governor, and my instincts had been right. Thankfully, Erik had, for once, listened to his little sister. "Arun is an idiot. I wasn't going to put Erik at risk like that, not for him. Not for anyone."

"Do you know where your brother is?"

"How would I? I've been underground for three days." That also wasn't a lie.

"There's something else—something I thought the elf might have told you to try to convince you to help him escape."

Done with the main course, I served myself a helping of cool, fresh fruit, a delicacy in Barepost. I thought I knew what he was going to say, but I couldn't give myself away, so I concentrated on peeling an orange slice.

"He has an airship. Do you know what that is?"

"Of course I do," I answered, though, of course, I hadn't known until Arun had told me.

"It's here, on Bruhier."

He was waiting for my reaction, but I didn't give him one. I just nodded, glad to be chewing so I didn't have to speak. I took the opportunity instead to turn his words over in my mind. So,

Luthair knew about the airship, and he knew where it was. He couldn't get to it, though, according to Arun. I just hoped Arun was right.

Luthair, fed up with my nonchalance, leaned forward, planting his hands on the table. "What did he tell you about the ship? If it's still here, I'm sure it's because he plans to escape in it."

"I already told you," I said, pushing my chair back. "Arun is an idiot. He didn't tell me about the ship, but maybe if he had, I wouldn't be sitting here now." I couldn't help taunting him a little.

Luthair smiled, regaining a bit of his composure as I lashed out at him. We were back in our typical pattern. "Well, I'll tell you this, in case you're considering looking for it. I have a surprise waiting for him, something he won't be prepared for."

There was a knock at the door, and Missus entered. In her hands, she carried my weapons belts, and with them, my ax and my sword. My heart soared at the sight.

Luthair glared at her, but before he could speak to send her away, I stood.

"That's good for you, governor. But let's get this straight. I don't care what you have planned for Arun Phina or his airship or his dragons." I put one last grape in my mouth, popping it between my teeth and letting the sweet and sour juice coat my tongue.

Then, I crossed the room to Missus and stood while she buckled on the belts. When she was done, she patted the ax at my hip and looked up at me, something like approval on her face.

"Oh, Svand," Luthair called. I turned. "I didn't say anything about dragons."

My breath caught in my throat when I realized my mistake. He would know I was lying, and if I lied about that, what else would he suspect me of? But I didn't get a chance to find out, because that was when a horrible scream tore through the room.

I shoved Missus behind me and put a hand to my weapon, spinning as I searched for the source of the noise.

Luthair, though, remained calm, and that was when I realized what I was hearing.

Not a scream.

An alarm.

An alarm I'd heard only once before, when the galestone had blown a hole in the mountainside. It was an alarm in the mines. What had Arun done?

Luthair was watching me, no longer smiling. "Do you have any idea what that's about?" he shouted over the sound.

"It's your mine." Then I was gone, out the front door before he could even think of a response.

CHAPTER 16

The streets were crammed with people, onlookers stepping out from their homes and their shops to look toward the mountain, shielding their eyes against the glare of the sun as they turned their gazes upward. But there was nothing to be seen. No smoke, no tumbling rocks, no quaking ground.

I shoved my way through them all, only one thing on my mind. Beating Luthair to Arun.

First, though, I had to convince my siblings.

The Gold Mine was empty except for four figures. Savarah, whom I had nearly forgotten about these last few days, leaned against the bar, Gerves behind her. Both of them watched Erik and Estrid, who stood in the middle of the room, squaring off against each other. It was a familiar scene, one I felt I had just witnessed not long ago between a sailor and a miner.

"You have to let it go," Estrid shouted in a tone that would make most men back down.

Not Erik. "Maybe you should have thought of that before you traded my life for my freedom," he shouted back at her. "I could even now be riding the stars with our mother, but—"

Estrid's eyes found mine where I stood in the doorway. She punched Erik sharply in the shoulder.

I felt like I had been punched, too, hearing them fight about the secret things I've stewed over for three years. The guilt and the shame that ate me up every time I watched Erik do Luthair's bidding. I knew Estrid felt it, too, but we never spoke about it, never acknowledged it. What could have possibly happened for it to bubble to the surface like this? For them to fight about it in public, in front of Savarah and Gerves.

I decided I didn't want to know, and even if I did want to throw my hat in the fight, now wasn't the time. "I thought you were in hiding."

"I was laying low." Erik looked tired, with his shoulders slumped and dark circles under his usually bright eyes. "But I heard the alarm. I had to come make sure you were okay."

"I'm fine, but you have to come with me."

"Where?" Erik asked. "Does this have anything to do with the elf?"

"Yes. We need to go, now. Up the cliffs. Arun Phina did something stupid, but we can help him."

"That was the alarm," Estrid said.

At the same time, Savarah made a small movement out of the corner of my eye, bringing her hand to a chain around her neck that I'd never noticed before.

When I turned, her face—typically covered with a bland smile—was openly astonished. "You found him?"

For all of her crowing about the Svands being the best, she had never really expected me to succeed. Not without my siblings, at least.

"Of course I did." I sneered, no longer pretending to be nice to her. "But you and your damned Tsarra Trisfina might as well have hired riders to announce your presence and your mission to Governor Luthair. It made things . . ." I paused and sighed for effect, "quite a bit more difficult."

Everyone was still for a breath.

Savarah slipped back behind her mask. She pulled two small throwing knives from her pockets, holding them expertly in her hands and smiled. "Well then, I suppose we'd better get a move on."

The alarm had stopped by the time we made it back outside, but the residents of Barepost were still crowded into the streets, gossiping about what could have happened. Some of them—the ones I suspected had family in the mines—looked worried and held each other in consolation. I wanted to stop and tell them not to worry, but we were racing against time now. I'd wasted too much time with Luthair and the detour to the pub.

We wove our way through the onlookers, and for once, Erik and Estrid followed me. I wasn't going in through the main entrance. Instead, I planned to somehow get out of Barepost past the sentries and then up the side of the cliff, where we would meet Arun on the other side of his escape.

Erik picked up his pace and began to walk beside me. "Frida, I can't—"

I gripped his arm. "He would have you spend the rest of your life in the mines. Or he would have me spend the rest of my life in his bed."

He looked stricken and didn't speak, but he kept moving, his eyes dropping to the ground.

"If we don't get out with Arun Phina now, it will be one or the other. It's time to give up your honor, forget the life-debt. Any reasonable man would have released you by now, and you know it."

He didn't have a chance to reply. We'd come to the gate, which was also the command center. It swarmed with Barepost guards in black uniform reporting to duty. We remained hidden behind a crumbling wall that had once belonged to an abandoned building. Most of the residences nearest to the gate had long been left behind by their owners, who'd grown weary of being on the front lines of any attack on the city. A majority of the guards were being dispatched to the inner town, either to the mine's main entrance or to control crowds downtown.

It did not seem like it would be too difficult to get past, and I was just turning to the others to debate a plan when there was a roar of commotion from the gate.

"Drop the bars," someone shouted over the din. "Man your stations."

I was no stranger to what that meant.

Barepost was under attack.

"We have to go," I said, "now." If we didn't make it past the gate before the bars that fortified the wall were dropped, we would be trapped. If we got out, though, who knew what Bruhier horror awaited us on the other side, drawn either by the sound of the alarm or by whatever Arun was doing on the other side of the mountain. What could it really be compared to the horror of staying in Barepost, though? It was a risk I, for one, was willing to take.

We made a mad, unorganized dash for the lowering gate, but even so, they didn't notice us until it was too late.

"Hey," someone I couldn't see shouted. "Stop them!"

The gate was halfway down when I dropped to my knees and crawled beneath, followed by Erik and Estrid, and finally Savarah, who barely made it, sliding through on her back with barely an inch to spare. The bars slammed into their iron bases, the guards safe on the other side. I watched them for a moment, trapped in their own prison, and they looked back, all of them wide-eyed with fear. Not for themselves, I realized. For us.

I turned and beheld . . .

What?

It was no monster I had ever seen before. A tree come to life. Its long body was covered in bark-like armor, and its branches were its arms and legs, sharpened to points that dug into the rock, cracking and spewing up bits of wood as they drove it forward. It wasn't made for climbing, which explained why we'd never seen it so high on the cliffs before. Its progress was slow, one step forward and a slide back, but it was still moving forward, still gaining ground.

But it wasn't coming for us or Barepost's gate. It was trailing two other figures, human in size and shape, up the side of the cliff just overhead. Two figures who, while obviously quick and strong, were not equipped to deal with it, barely able to keep out of reach of its pincers. If they had made it to Barepost before the bars came down, they would have stood a chance, but now . . .

"We can help them," Erik said, his hand already on his sword.

"Or we can use them as bait," Savarah offered, that bland, secret smile on her face as if she were enjoying watching the two struggle. "Keep it distracted while we get around to the other side."

Estrid tilted her head as if considering the idea, her eyes also on the pair.

I, on the other hand, had already resigned myself to what we had to do. I knew that the guards in Barepost wouldn't bother attacking the monster. They didn't want to draw its attention. We were the only hope for these two mysterious stragglers.

I looked at Erik. "Let's go."

We ran along the hill's edge at first, Savarah trailing behind. I understood her reluctance. We were so close to completing Tsarra's task, so close to rescuing Arun Phina. But if she knew Arun at all, she would know that this would be what he would choose too. What were two more passengers on the *Iron Duchess* anyway? Arun wanted to save them all, right? I surprised myself by wishing Arun were here, knowing he would be pleased.

When we reached the edge of the hill where it met the mountain, Erik, Estrid, and I buckled ourselves onto one another. We were used to the climb and were well equipped. We were quick, knowing that every moment wasted brought the pair above us closer to death.

Erik turned to Savarah. "You're with me." He pulled her flush against him, his big arm around her narrow waist.

Her mask slipped for only the second time since I'd met her, her face twisting into shock at his boldness.

Estrid turned quickly away, her lips pressed together to hold in her amusement, and began to climb.

It didn't matter how many times we'd done it, climbing up a sheer rock wall was no easy task. Not to mention this was a different part of the mountain than we were used to, without our well-worn handholds. And Erik was almost entirely supporting Savarah. I made a silent vow then that if she did something stupid to get us pulled down, I would cut her away to fall to her own death. But we all had our hand-picks strapped to our wrists and a basic knowledge of where not to put our feet, so we made quick progress.

Estrid got to the monster first, just as it reached the pair, who had taken refuge on a small ledge. A big man with dark hair covering half of his face was trying to fend it off with his sword, but the monster's bark-like shell made it nearly impenetrable. Their only saving grace was that it kept sliding down whenever it picked up a leg to skewer them. There was a girl with him. She carried a long spear and was trying to thrust it forward, but the man kept pushing her back behind him. If there was one rule about fighting on the cliffs, it was never stop climbing. If there was another rule, it was stay out of reach. They had broken both, and it wouldn't be long before they paid dearly for it.

Estrid's sword struck one of the back legs. Startled, the monster's leg shot out, connecting with Estrid's face and knocking her backward. Her hand-pick came loose, and she slid several feet. I braced myself, pressing my body against the wall, and felt the rope at my waist go taut as it held her.

"Are you all right?" I asked, glancing down.

She didn't answer. She was already climbing back up.

I was doing my best not to get in the way of the back limb near me that flailed and slid wildly on the rocks, carving deep grooves and sending splinters raining over us. What could we use to kill a tree?

I looked down at my brother who was just below me, Savarah hanging onto his back. "Do you still have the galestone?"

He lifted himself up another arm's length. "Better than that." He reached inside of his leather vest. "I have this." He pulled out what I recognized as Gerves's galestone pistol.

I wasn't sure that was truly better, though it could be more effective. If it worked. If it didn't blow my face off. "Why do you have that?"

"Gerves's parting gift," he answered with a smile.

"Well, we have to be smart about it."

"Aren't we always?"

I didn't want to answer that. So instead, I took the pistol from him while he withdrew a packet with a metal ball and galestone powder. Each of us using one hand, we loaded the pistol, Savarah watching over Erik's shoulder. Estrid had joined us too. Blood dripped from her nose, but she didn't seem to notice.

"Aim," Erik said.

I did, pointing the iron nose of the pistol at the back of the monster's slender, wooden head. Watching it, seeing it reach and stretch its branch arms for the pair on the ledge, I wondered how many of these I'd unknowingly passed in the forests of Bruhier. How many I had walked near, how many I had rested against. All these years, and none had made themselves known to us. So why now? What had these two done to incur its wrath?

Thunder rumbled overhead, barely audible over the

monster's thrashing, and I remembered what Erik had said about galestone not lighting in the rain.

"Hurry," I said as he struggled with the flint.

He struck it against the rock once, twice, and finally, a spark. It caught on the fuse sticking out of the back of the pistol's barrel and began burning.

"Aim," Erik repeated.

I squinted, pointing the pistol at the back of the monster's head, and begged Oya for a straight, clean shot.

The pistol grew warm in my hands as the fire traveled into the barrel. Erik braced my elbow, and suddenly, the world exploded. Fire raced out of my hands, tracing a burning path along the creature's back. The ball buried itself in his head, smoke streaming out of the small hole, followed by licking flames. The monster thrashed and screamed, and in its pain, forgot itself. Forgot that it wasn't safe on the ground, roots buried deep, sleeping its eternal slumber. Forgot that it was hundreds of feet in the air, hanging off the side of a cliff. And it let go.

I pressed myself against the rock but still, branches whipped at my face and scratched my hands.

"No!" Erik shouted.

My first thought was Estrid, but she was beside me. I twisted, looking down, and saw him holding Savarah by only her hand, the rest of her dangling precariously off the cliff. Even worse, Erik was barely hanging on to his hand-pick himself, the hand grasping it bloody and trembling.

Estrid moved toward him, sliding sideways until she was close enough to wrap a hand in the fabric of his tunic. "Pull her up."

Erik grimaced. "Don't you think I would if I could?"

"Then let her go." Estrid widened her eyes at our brother as if that were the obvious answer.

"I—"

"Now is not the time for bickering," I yelled.

Estrid huffed and let go of Erik, reaching down to grab onto Savarah's other hand. Together, they hauled her up between them. Both of them hung on by one hand, and I could feel them slowly shifting their weight to the ropes strapped to my belt. My arms, already sore from days in the mine, shook.

But I could not let go. Would not let go. Too many people were counting on me. "Let's go. One step at a time."

That was what we did, each of us moving our picks one at a time, crawling up the mountainside. Overhead, the two strangers peered down at us, neither of them speaking.

When we were closer, the man lay down on the ledge and leaned over, the woman behind him, bracing his legs. "Just a little farther."

I stretched, reaching for him just as the tree monster had done. The man's hand clapped around my forearm and dragged me forward over the ledge. "I cannot thank you enough—" He stopped, studying my face.

Estrid and Erik joined us, followed by Savarah, all of us squeezing onto the ledge, everyone watching this man.

His companion peeked out from behind him but did not speak.

Thunder rumbled overhead.

A drop of rain hit my face. "Who are—"

I drew up short when the man raised a finger and pointed at my face. "Suun?"

Before I could say anything, Estrid turned to Erik. "Where's Savarah?"

Erik turned as if she were hiding behind him but came up empty. "She was just here. I thought . . . Did she make it over the ledge? Did she . . ."

She had, I knew she had. I'd seen her stand, watched her brush her skirts off and pull her hair back from her face. And then . . . I gasped, a hand covering my mouth.

The three of us peered over. Below us, the tree monster lay in shattered remains, branches and sticks and roots scattered in pieces that made it unrecognizable for what it had once been. Now it was just firewood. But there was no evidence of Savarah. She was just . . .

Gone.

CHAPTER 17

I stood, turning to the new members of our group just as the rain fell in earnest. We huddled together beneath the ledge's small overhang.

"Who are you, and what are you doing here?" I asked, squinting at them.

Estrid and Erik were beside me, one on each side, and I was sure we made an intimidating picture.

But neither of the newcomers backed down.

"I am Beru," the man said, still looking at me strangely, as if he knew me from somewhere, though I had never seen him before in my life. "This is Aria." He gestured to the woman, offering no clue as to their relationship.

She raised a hand in greeting. "We were on a journey but were waylaid by . . ." She looked down, then back up at us. "Whatever that was. Can you help us get to safety?"

I shrugged. "It will come at a cost. To reach safety, you'll have to climb. And fight." I didn't know if they would make it, but I certainly didn't want to send them back down to Barepost.

"More of the same, then," the man—Beru—grumbled.

"We can do it." Aria looked sideways at her companion. "We've come this far."

"A fool's errand."

I rolled my eyes, turning away from them, not interested in adding their problems to my own. The rain had already stopped, leaving the ledge slick but passable. "Let's go." We'd wasted enough time. Probably too much time.

There was a small, barely-there path that wound up from the ledge and around the side of the cliff, and we followed it with small, shuffling steps, me in the lead. I knew we had to be getting close, and sure enough, after a few minutes, I heard voices.

The miners came into view not long after. The hole Arun and I had found was, from the outside, barely visible. I would have missed it if not for the men gathered on a large, flat outcropping of rock. I spotted Owin and Bertol, and several others whose names I hadn't learned in the last few days. But no Arun.

I hailed the men, who looked startled at my sudden appearance. One even held his pickax up as if to throw it at me, but Bertol stilled his hand.

"Where is Arun?" I asked. We'd reached a gap in our path, so I had to yell across, unable to get any closer.

Bertol pointed to the hole. "Helping."

That was when Xalph emerged from the hole, pulling himself through with his scrawny arms. He blinked once, twice, and then tumbled out into Owin's waiting arms. Even though the man was missing a hand, he gathered Xalph up tightly and helped him to his feet. I should have been moving, climbing across, helping Beru and Aria, but I couldn't seem to take my eyes off of Xalph. He toed the very edge of the rock on which he stood and gazed out after the vast landscape. I tried to imagine it as he saw it—the size of the world, the brightness of it all, after being trapped beneath the ground for his entire life.

"Frida," Erik said from behind me, "we have to keep going."

He was right. Using my hand-picks, I made my way across the gap in the path, then reached back for Aria and then Beru in turn. The man begrudgingly accepted my help, then ushered Aria toward the miners, obviously glad to have other company. Erik and Estrid crossed with no issue, but Erik still accepted my hand when I held it out to him.

"I'm sorry," he said, voice low enough that only I could hear, "that you felt like you had to do this for us."

"It's not just for us." I motioned to the group, to Xalph.

Erik nodded and patted me on the shoulder, then approached Bertol to introduce himself. I didn't know if he understood how much that small bit of approval meant to me.

Then Arun appeared, tumbling through the opening and rolling to his feet. He was dirty as ever, his hair loose from its strap, tumbling around his shoulders. There was a bloody gash on one arm, but he didn't pay it any attention.

"That's it," he said to no one in particular. "There's no one else." Then he saw me and went still, his face cautious and guarded.

He didn't know, I realized, whether I was there to help him or to hunt him for Luthair. "You made it."

He shrugged, as if it were no small feat. "So did you."

I looked back at the hole, expecting to see a platoon of guards scrambling through, but it was quiet. "What did you do?"

"A cave in."

That explained the alarm.

"We trapped ourselves inside the tunnel. On purpose."

"So while they're on the inside trying to free you . . ."

"We're out here, freeing ourselves."

I nodded, slightly impressed in spite of myself. "I was with Luthair today. He suspects your plan to get to your airship. He says he has a surprise waiting for you."

Arun exhaled, his eyes scanning the miners on the ledge.

"That should be exciting. Let's get there first, and then we'll worry about whatever he has planned."

The miners were armed with only their pickaxes, brute strength, and stubborn determination, but it seemed to be enough. We were a strange parade as we hauled ourselves up the mountain, me and my siblings bringing up the rear. Owin and Xalph were between Arun and some of the other stronger men, helped along one painful step at a time. Aria and Beru were holding their own in spite of being ill-equipped for the climb.

Arun pointed to a ledge a few yards overhead, gesturing that we should head for it.

Another break, another chance for Luthair to catch us. But we had to do what was best for the group.

We shifted our trajectory for the outcropping, and then, as the first man reached it, I heard the scream. It was a sound that usually sent the people of Barepost running for cover, a sound that drew archers to their posts. The sound echoed off the rocks and bounced around in my head.

It took everything I had to remember not to let go and cover my ears. I looked up, knowing exactly what I would see.

The dreadwing had a face that made a mockery of the human visage, the nose morphed into a sharp beak, the lips pulled back to bare rows of sharp teeth. Its legs were long and muscled, ending in finger-like talons. The neck was ruffled and thick, and the back was hunched between two huge feathered wings that it had in place of arms. It was one of the only flying monsters we had encountered in Bruhier, and one of the worst, despite it being one of the smallest. They didn't attack frequently, but when they did, it almost always ended in death.

Erik looked at me, his face grim. There was nothing we could do except keep going. Men scrambled onto the ledge, pulling up their friends and preparing to fight off the beast if needed. But it just hovered, drawing long, lazy circles with its shadow. Waiting, I thought, for the perfect moment.

It drew nearer to us, and I took a warning swing at it with one of my hand-axes. It snarled at me and skittered away. That was when I realized we weren't moving.

A few yards away and overhead, Xalph was frozen. Owin urged him forward, but there was only so much he could do with one hand. Xalph trembled, pressing himself against the rock and shaking his head.

"Xalph!" I hissed. "Go!"

The dreadwing smelled weakness and saw its chance. It dove for Xalph. The men on the ledge shouted. Owin tried to figure out how to reach for him.

Estrid moved quickly, sidestepping and climbing at the same time.

But I was frozen. None of us would make it on time. The beast was on Xalph, its talons digging into a skinny shoulder.

Xalph cried out and released the wall to beat at the bird, too late realizing his mistake. I saw from my place below him the moment he knew he would fall, the fear and shock on his face.

Then Owin reached for the boy.

Arun had a hold of his other arm, fingers wrapped around the crook of his elbow like a handle. Arun grunted as he took all of the man's weight.

The dreadwing tore at Xalph, trying to tug him away from Owin's iron grip, but the man would not let go, his face red with effort.

"Owin!" Arun cried, and I knew the monster had won.

The miner's arm was jerked out of Arun's hands as the dreadwing lifted Xalph off the wall, trailing Owin behind him like a bonus prize. But the weight was too much, and rather than fall to its death, it released Xalph. I hardly had time to think, but I knew instinctively what I had to do.

"Whatever you do," I shouted to Erik and Estrid, "don't let go."

And then I threw myself off the wall.

I caught Xalph under the arms. He was still holding Owin, and together, tethered by the ropes at my belt attached to my siblings, we swung back against the cliff. I shielded him with my body, taking the brunt of the blow, but there was nothing I could do for Owin, who hit it just as hard as I did.

Erik and Estrid struggled.

I had to right myself, had to pull it together as soon as possible. They couldn't hold us forever.

"Frida," Xalph said, my name a groan instead of a yell.

I looked down at him and saw that he had Owin with two hands, but he was still slipping.

"Erik! Quick!"

"Frida." There was something in Erik's voice that made me look up. When I did, he pointed at something.

A fray in the rope.

"It won't hold."

Panicked, I looked at Xalph, then at Owin. "Can you climb to the ledge?" I asked Owin.

The miner had also seen the rope, and I saw him measure the distance to the ledge with his eyes. There was no way and he knew it.

"Keep him safe. He belongs to all of us."

"Owin, no!" Xalph shouted.

But Owin had already freed himself, slipping his hand out of Xalph's grip. He fell silently.

Xalph screamed.

I had no time to be hurt or scared or angry. I swung Xalph, who was light now, up to Estrid, and then took Erik's offered hand as he helped me right myself. I dug my hand-axes into the rock with maybe a little too much force, surprised to feel a tear on the side of my nose.

"I'm sorry," Erik said.

I hurriedly wiped my face on my shirt. "It's fine."

Owin had given his hand for Xalph, and then his life. For Xalph, who was nobody to him. Not his son, not his brother. But he'd loved him that fiercely anyway—enough to die for him. I knew then that Erik would do the same, no matter how foolhardy or irrational or scared I was. Erik would lay down his life for me. It didn't matter who my mother was or was not. But I hoped he would never have to.

Xalph and I were the last to reach the ledge.

Arun held Xalph tight to him before pulling me over and unexpectedly doing the same. His chest was firm and large, and it felt safe. Like the dreadwing or the memories of Owin's face in his final moment couldn't reach me here.

I fought back tears, wiping my eyes on his dirty shirt before pulling away. "What was that for?"

Only Estrid watched us, her eyebrows squeezed together.

"You know what," Arun said. "Thank you."

I didn't deserve his gratitude. "I'm sorry I couldn't save him. Or Savarah," I added, thinking of both their bodies broken and lifeless on the forest floor.

"Who?"

The other men were already working their way up the mountain again, eager to reach the top, to leave the tragedy behind.

"Savarah," I repeated. "Tsarra's friend. Her 'trusted advisor.'"

Arun shrugged, hoisting Xalph up the wall. Estrid had taken off her belt and given it to Xalph, belting him to Erik, who went next. "I don't know any Savarah."

A few yards away, Beru was helping Aria up, and his eyes caught mine. He looked startled as if the name maybe meant something to him, but he didn't say anything. Something felt . . . off. But I didn't have time to linger on it. Now wasn't the time to discuss social connections anyway.

"Shall we go?" Arun gestured to the wall.

"Go ahead," I said, distracted as I hooked up my own belt.

"Ladies first."

I cut my eyes at him, trying to see if he was joking.

He looked back with a straight face, his eyes dark beneath their heavy brows. I wondered what he saw when he looked at me. What he felt.

I pushed those thoughts away and took my place on the wall, burying the ax in to support my weight. We were moving faster now, the excitement of the group palpable, and when I tilted my head back to look up, I knew why.

The top of the world was finally in sight.

Freedom and the future I longed for were very nearly in my reach.

I didn't know what exactly I'd expected to find on top of the plateau, but it wasn't guards dressed in Luthair's black uniform, swords and bows at the ready. Or a wooden pike fence, several feet tall without an ally in sight.

Arun and I had walked the perimeter, keeping to the trees that circled the clearing where he said his airship was docked. Guards were stationed every few feet. There was no break in the fence and no gate except for the one in front of us now, and guards swarmed around it. I had no doubt in my mind that they knew we were coming.

Arun and I both ducked out of sight, our backs against a fallen tree trunk several feet wide. I didn't want to think about what might have knocked it over, and whether or not any of the seemingly benign trees were really monsters waiting to come to life.

"I suppose this is my surprise." Arun wiped a hand down his face.

I smiled meekly at him and patted his hand. "He wouldn't be Luthair if he didn't make us miserable one last time." It was optimistic to think this was the last time, but he didn't correct me.

We dropped back to where the rest of the group was hunched in a small cave near the edge of the plateau.

Bertol comforted Xalph and some of the other men from his group.

Aria and Beru stood a few feet from them with Erik and Estrid, none of them having known Owin.

Arun and I squeezed in with them, keeping our voices low.

"It's not good," I confirmed.

"Of course it's not." Estrid put an arm around my shoulder to lessen the blow of her disappointment.

"But not impossible."

"We have the numbers," Beru said, gesturing to the group of miners.

Arun shook his head. "They aren't fighters. They're old or out of shape or injured. It's just us." He pointed to the six of us. "Which is more than Luthair was counting on, I'm sure of it."

He was right. Luthair would expect Arun and a bunch of exhausted prisoners. Not Arun with three D'ahvol and two mystery warriors. But it still wasn't enough, not against a whole squadron. We needed something else . . . we needed . . .

"Remember the blazetaur?" I asked suddenly, interrupting Arun who had been running down the numbers and the layout of the fence.

Erik and Estrid both nodded while the other three looked on blankly.

"What exactly are you thinking?" Erik asked.

I smiled. "Distraction."

Estrid breathed heavily through her nose and glanced around at the others. "She means bait."

We waited until the sun was low enough to cast long, dark shadows across the ground, and made our move.

Aria had been the obvious choice to be the bait in question.

A beautiful stranger would lower the guards' alert level quicker than anything else I could think of. And it made sense to head straight for the front gate. While other areas of the fence were less heavily guarded, it would take too long to get everyone over the fence. We would just have to fight and hope that Aria would provide us with enough of a head start that we would stand a chance.

Though they tried to follow my instructions and make as little noise as possible, the group of escapees sounded—to me at least—as loud as a blazetaur barreling through the forest, trampling everything in its path. I was relieved when the fence came into view and they could stop moving, all of them taking cover behind the fallen tree, the dark and the shadows making it easier to hide them.

"Are you sure you want to do this?" Beru asked Aria, his hands on her shoulders.

But Aria was no withering female needing him to hold her up. She shook him off. "Yes. I'd do anything to get off this island."

I understood her sentiment.

Aria and I went to the edge of the trees and looked at the fence. They'd lit torches along the fence perimeter, creating a circle of light. There were four guards outside the guardhouse by the gate.

"Those are your guys."

Aria didn't say anything but threw her shoulders back, took a deep breath, and plunged forward, stumbling out of the tree line. I almost reached for her, convinced by her act before I remembered that it was all part of the game. I just didn't know she'd be so good at it.

"Help! Thank Onen! Please help!"

"Who's there?" A guard swung his bow in her direction.

She was undeterred. She stopped a few yards away and fell to her knees. "Please, come quick. My sister—"

He and his companions lowered their weapons, and one even knelt before Aria, a hand on her shoulder.

"Girl? What is it?"

"My sister," Aria wailed, waving a hand at the trees. At me. I ducked behind a tree trunk as the guards' eyes scanned the tree line. "She's— A monster— Oh!"

"What's going on out there?" A man's voice came from the guardhouse, a figure emerging in the square light from the open door.

"It's a girl," said one of the guards.

Aria wailed loudly as if to prove it.

"She says there's someone in the woods."

"Well, go check it out," ordered the man from the guardhouse. The four men peered into the darkness. Then they gathered their weapons and stepped around Aria.

She pushed herself to her feet and followed.

"Where is she?" one of the guards asked. "Your sister." There were at least five of them following her and one lurking outside of the guardhouse, watching with interest.

I followed, quiet as a mouse through the underbrush. It was the hunt, the anticipation, the rush of adrenaline—this was what I loved. Next would come the fight, and I loved that too.

"Just over there," Aria pointed vaguely in the direction of a tree stump nearby, just outside of the circle of light.

It was there that Estrid lay in wait. It had taken some convincing to get her to play the injured sister, but when she learned that she wouldn't miss out on any of the action, she'd accepted her role.

And she was disturbingly good at it. She lay with her long limbs splayed haphazardly around her, her hair half-covering her face. What they couldn't see were the small knives cupped in her palms. They couldn't see me or Arun or Beru or Erik, all lying in wait. They couldn't see that this was the end of this life for them.

One bent over Estrid, not touching her. "Where is she hurt?"

Another man came close, both of them bending to inspect her.

Aria did not have to make up a response, because it was then that Estrid's arms lashed out, her hands sliding across the men's throats.

At first, they didn't realize what had happened.

The rest of us attacked, each of us taking out one of the guards as silently and as quickly as possible. The man closest to me was short and carried a galestone pistol at his hip that he hadn't even drawn. That was how green Luthair's men were. I stepped out of the shadows, wrapped a hand around his mouth, and drew the very edge of the ax blade across his throat, making the cut deep enough that he could not scream and alert the others.

He turned, his hands wrapped around his throat, his eyes meeting mine.

I wondered only briefly who he was and who would miss him when he did not come home. He dropped to his knees, blood seeping between his fingers. There was a sound when a man died, a gentle exhalation as if of relief as his spirit passed from this world to the next. I heard it then as his face went slack and he collapsed to the ground.

Looking around, I saw that the others had also been successful in felling their marks, though Erik stood to the side without any blood on his hands. He had his arms crossed over his chest and was glaring at Estrid as she picked herself up off the ground, shoving a body away from her as she did.

"You had to do them both?" He scowled. "You make me look like a weakling."

But Estrid just smiled. "I didn't know how many there were. And besides, you weren't the one lying there with their horrid breath in your face."

Erik was still grumbling as he began to strip the bigger of

the two men of his uniform. Not far from him, Arun was doing the same but paused, kneeling to pick up a longbow that had fallen from the guard's shoulders, weighing it in his hand and smiling.

Beru watched him, then looked at the corpse at his feet. The guard's eyes were open, staring at the sky. "I don't know about this. It seems disrespectful of the dead."

"Well," I said, grunting as I pulled my own guard's arms out of his tunic and vest. "They were disrespectful of my life, so . . ."

"Hear, hear." Estrid was already dressing, covering her normal earth-tone leathers with the black linen of the guard's uniform.

When we were all dressed—even Beru—it was hard to tell us apart, especially once we pulled the hoods up to cover our hair. Arun was mostly excited about the bow. He kept reaching over his shoulder and touching its upper limb and smiling. I thought I knew how he felt when Missus had strapped on my weapons belts earlier that day and returned my ax to me. I had no use for my guard's galestone pistol so I left it lying on the ground.

"Do you know how to use that thing?" I asked, dropping back to walk beside him as we made our way back to the fence.

He cut his eyes at me. I tucked a strand of hair behind my ear, acutely aware of its roundness in his presence. Some D'ahvol had more pointed ears because of our elven lineage, but not me—my ears were completely human.

"In the Phina family, when the children come of age, they are sent to the forest and not allowed to return until they've carved a bow and fashioned three arrows complete with the fletching of a raptor owl's feathers."

"How long were you gone?" I asked.

He smiled wide, showing off the dimples on either cheek. "I don't know if I ever truly returned. In a way, I am still gone."

The six of us emerged out of the tree line, blinking into the circle of light made by the watchmen's torches. A figure cast in silhouette still stood in the door to the guardhouse.

"Well?" he shouted across the small clearing. "Did you find her? Where are they?"

"We could not save them," Erik answered, his voice low to hide his Ahvoli accent.

He let us approach without a hint of suspicion, holding the door open for us to enter. As he passed, Erik leaned close to him as if to tell him a secret, and next thing I knew, the guard was toppling forward, his mouth open in shock. Erik caught him and lowered him silently to the ground. Then we filed inside the guardhouse and dispatched the rest of the men there. They'd been on break, gathered around a card table, and that was where they died their dishonorable deaths.

When none of Luthair's men at the gate were left standing, we began to usher in the rest of the group. They ran past us quickly and quietly, disappearing into the shadows beyond the gate. According to Arun, the airship was not far away, maybe a quarter mile, docked near a cluster of three boulders. That was their destination. Xalph was bringing up the rear with Bertol.

"That's the last of us," Xalph confirmed.

"Hey!"

We all turned and saw a man standing there.

I squinted at him, thinking his features familiar.

It was the guard who had delivered me to Luthair after the fight on the *Gem*. "What's going on here?"

I felt Arun come up behind me. "Refugees," he said, which was stupid because Luthair would never allow refugees onto his land.

The guard knew it too. He turned and ran at the same time he began yelling. "Breach! They're here! The elf is here!"

Arun lifted his bow, notching an arrow before I could blink and aiming it at the man's back. He was so close that I heard the twang of the string as he let it go. The arrow flew straight and true, piercing the guard through his back and silencing him. But it was already too late. I saw the warning fires going up along the top of the fence as the guards lit them to summon the others. Any minute now, we would be overrun with Luthair's men.

"Go," I urged Xalph and Bertol, who were the only non-fighting men left. "Get to the ship and hide. Wait for Arun."

"And you," Xalph said.

I nodded. "All of us." I certainly didn't have any plans to be left behind.

My siblings joined me as we faced the open gate, Beru and Aria to our right, Arun behind us, his bow held aloft.

"It was a good plan," Erik said, the only one of us to speak. "While it lasted."

It wasn't another minute before the first guards rounded the corner.

Arun let more arrows fly. He dropped three men before they realized what was happening and took cover behind the fence and inside the guardhouse.

"Cowards!" Estrid shouted, brandishing her sword as an invitation to anyone who wanted to parry.

A guard hung his head out the window of the guard-house and aimed a galestone pistol at us, getting off only one wild shot before Arun buried an arrow in his throat. There was the sound of another shot from inside the house as if the pistol had discharged accidentally. Then we saw the flames, orange fingers spreading quickly through the house.

"If any of them have any galestone—" Erik started, but I already knew what he was going to say.

"Run." I shoved Arun to the side and we fell, rolling in a tangle of limbs to take cover behind a tree just as the house exploded.

The heat from the fire consumed us, and I worried for a

second that we weren't far enough away, but then it subsided, and I could breathe again.

"Onen save me," Arun said a little breathlessly from where he had fallen beneath me.

We didn't have time to catch our breath, though. The remaining guards, the ones who hadn't been in the guardhouse —which was a raging inferno now, black smoke billowing into the sky and tall orange flames acting as a beacon for any monster searching for a late night snack—came rushing around the corner, taking advantage of our distraction and momentary panic. But our crew met them without any hesitation, Estrid and Erik grinning from ear to ear. Even Beru joined the fray, his face grim but his fighting moves flawless.

A guard with two swords was the first to approach me. He did not gloat or seem excited about it.

Well, at least he would die a smart man.

He was fast, pushing forward strong and quick, but I was ready for him. Metal met metal in a flurry of blades that flashed in the firelight, but it was only a matter of moments before I caught both of his swords with mine, and my ax slipped past, lodging itself in his side. My hand, stitched and bandaged though it was, did not cause me any problems, apparently.

I jerked the ax back out in a spray of blood. He looked down at the wound and then back at me, shock in his eyes.

His swords clanged loudly against each other as he dropped them, then he collapsed onto his side. I knelt, picking up one of the blades and wrapping his hands around its hilt.

"Go with your ancestors." The old words came back to me. I didn't know what he believed or where he would go in the next life, but I figured it was better than nothing. "May your spirit join with those who have gone before you."

"Does the monster have a heart, then?" came a voice from behind.

I stood, raising my weapons and turning to face—

Jesper.

I laughed.

His face turned red with rage.

"Your nose still looks a little crooked. It's quite the improvement."

He growled and lunged, quicker than I would have thought, but his anger made him sloppy. Luckily, I had been trained my whole life on how to channel that anger into steady control. I knocked his sword away and side-stepped, letting him stumble past.

"I could do this all night," I taunted.

He regained his footing and turned to me again. His sword met mine with surprising force that knocked me back a step. I parried, and when he swung his shield at my head, I ducked. He'd left himself wide open, but my ax met air as he maneuvered away, putting space between us. I grimaced at him.

He laughed. "What? Did you think it would be easy?"

I cocked my head at him. "Do you think this is hard?"

Estrid appeared over his shoulder. She cut down two men with one swing of her sword.

I was done playing with Jesper. He and Aysche had never shown me any mercy. I certainly wasn't going to show him any. I hoisted my ax up to my shoulder, my fingers loose around the hilt, the movement more instinctual than anything. It was still wet with the other man's blood, the red liquid coating my fingers, and the once-white bandage that was wrapped around my palm was stained brown. Before Jesper even realized that I wasn't playing by his rules, that I was done with the swordplay and the verbal sparring, I'd let the ax go. It buried itself between his eyes, just above his healing nose, and he fell backward, dead in an instant.

CHAPTER 19

I should have been happy, but instead, I just felt a sick twisting in my gut and thought for a horrifying moment that I might throw up. I'd been in fights before, spilled blood before, taken lives before, but they'd never meant anything. They'd never been personal.

Estrid ran by, slapping me on the shoulder, effectively shaking me out of my stupor. She was excited, her cheeks flushed, bouncing on her toes. "That felt good, didn't it? It's been too long." She spotted my ax in Jesper's face and pulled it out.

I had just been planning on leaving it there, even if it was my most prized possession. I didn't want to look into his face again.

She handed me the ax.

I flexed my fingers on my sore hand and then took it from her, tucking it into my belt.

Arun approached at a trot. "That's the last of them." He turned around, beckoning to us. "Let's go. Let's find the others and get off this island."

We'd left carnage behind us only to find more of it when we reached the *Iron Duchess*. Bodies were scattered around the ship in a gruesome circle, but it was no one I knew. No one who had come with us up the cliff.

No, here were Arun's dragon friends, every last one of them dead.

"What is this?" Estrid rolled one green-scaled body over to reveal a gaping wound in its belly.

Arun spun in a circle, looking at his friends' bodies. "I never —" He paused, choking on his words.

Erik was at another body, this one larger and covered in red scales. Its leathery wings were torn to shreds. "Dragons. Incredible." It was then that I saw he was holding one of his arms close to his side, his other hand wrapped around the bicep.

I crossed to him. "What happened?" I turned him to face me. He was covered in blood, his face and hands and clothing dirty and torn.

"Just a scratch."

I pulled his hand away. It wasn't just a scratch. His left arm was badly burned, the skin raw and red. "The explosion."

"I'll be fine."

Aria appeared then. She studied his arm and gingerly touched the burn.

Erik winced.

"I can help. I'm sure there are medical kits on board."

"Erik—" I started.

Aria looked back at me. "I was a healer in an earlier life."

I didn't know her, but for some reason, felt I could trust her. "Fine. Let me know if you need me."

They boarded the ship, and I turned around, searching for Arun, finding him near the edge of the trees, far away from any of the discarded dragon bodies.

He'd dropped into a squat, burying his face in his hands.

I approached, putting a hand on his back. It was warm and solid, and I could just feel the gentle beating of his heart against my palm. "It's not your fault."

"So many have died . . ." He didn't look up at me.

I squatted next to him, ducking my head to try to look him in the eyes. "And so many will live because of it."

He looked up then. "Not because of it. In spite of it. In spite of all my stupid decisions and damned pride."

"Hey." I pulled his hands into mine. My right hand was still crusted with a dead man's blood. "Your stupid decisions and damned pride have also saved people. They saved me. Erik. Estrid. Xalph. Bertol. You can sit here and feel sorry for yourself"—I squeezed his hands to emphasize my point—"or you can get up and finish what you started. I might be able to do a lot, but I can't fly a ship."

He took a deep, cleansing breath and together we stood, turning to face the *Iron Duchess*.

The ship itself was a marvel, more magnificent than even the *Green Gem,* Luthair's prized possession, but also obviously very different, even to a landlubber's eye. The body of the ship was crafted from a dark, rich wood, and shaped like a sky whale. It even had strange wing-like sails hanging off the sides and the back as if they were the whale's flippers and flukes. It had four tall masts and a fan of sails hanging loosely from the one in front, attached to the bowsprit. While I was admiring this marvel, Arun was murmuring under his breath. He approached the ship and hoisted one of the flipper-like sails.

It collapsed back to the ground with a groan.

"What is it?"

He took a step back and looked up at the deck, then the masts, a hand over his eyes. "He destroyed her. He must not have been able to figure out how to get her in the air, so he . . ." He waved a hand at the ship and then I saw what I had not before—the booms snapped in half and hanging limply from the masts, their sails with long tears in them.

I followed Arun on deck, where the damage was even more obvious. Floorboards had been ripped up, railings smashed, and the beautiful wooden wheel had been torn away from the helm. Arun ignored all of these. Instead, he crossed the deck to the mainmast and gave it a tug as if testing its sturdiness. Then he began to climb.

I turned away as Erik and Estrid emerged from the crew's quarters, some of the others behind them. Erik's arm was bandaged from wrist to elbow in a clean white cloth, and the color had returned to his face.

I would have to thank Aria, but she didn't give me the chance. As soon as she emerged, she scrambled after Arun. I didn't know if she had experience with these airships, but maybe she could help. She'd certainly earned my trust, after all.

Beru watched her for a moment and then turned to me, his eyes studying my face.

Erik and Estrid followed me off the ship, and Beru followed them. From our spot on solid ground, we turned to watch Arun scale the mast using these small, wooden posts as a tenuous ladder.

Xalph and Bertol were on the deck with some of the other miners, picking up scraps of wood and making a debris pile in the middle of the deck.

"If this thing doesn't fly," Estrid said, "we're done for. There's no way we can go back to Barepost now. Not after what we did here."

"It will be the perfect excuse for Luthair to throw us into the mines," Erik added.

What it was, I thought but didn't say, was the perfect excuse for him to hold marriage over my head again, use our freedom from the mines as a bargaining chip. He had to know I would do it. "Arun will get her up in the air."

"Her?" Erik asked with a small smile. "You're starting to sound like him."

At the edge of the forest, just beyond the shadowy tree line, I saw movement. My hand went to my ax, but then the creature emerged into the clearing.

A griffin. While certainly not harmless, they were definitely one of the more peaceful creatures on Bruhier. We'd encountered only a few in our time on the island, since they seemed to prefer to live as high as possible, on plateau tops and above the veil. He studied our group with his black bird eyes, pronged tail twitching. Then it leapt onto the tallest of the three nearby boulders and sat, the muscles in its powerful, cat-like haunches bunching together, its front bird-like claws digging into the dirt.

It arched its feathered neck back and yawned mightily, revealing rows of sharp teeth inside a black beak. There was a white band around its eyes that made its face practically shine in the moonlight. Xalph had spotted it and was leaning over the railing, gesturing to it and talking excitedly to Bertol, who was smiling, his hands in his pockets.

You don't have to kill everything that has claws.

Right. I took my hand off my ax and turned back to Erik and Estrid.

"A female." Erik was also studying the creature. "You can tell by her smaller size."

"We could still say we weren't involved." Estrid darted her eyes from the griffin back to us, as disinterested in it as it was in her. "I don't think anyone who has seen us has lived. We could just . . . go back and pretend none of this happened."

"I would sooner kiss a griffin than do that."

Erik chuckled and clapped a hand on my shoulder, squeezing gently. "You might have your opportunity."

The griffin looked on from her spot several yards away, unamused.

Beru watched the exchange. I could feel his eyes on my face. It took an incredible amount of restraint not to bring my hand up to cover the mark beside my eye. Though I should have been used to it by now, it still bothered me when people stared at it. Instead, I turned my attention back to the ship. Arun had reached the crow's nest now, Aria not far behind him. It was intact, as if Luthair's men couldn't be bothered to climb that high. He pulled himself inside and lifted up on his toes to reach a blue box above the crow's nest, nearly at the top of the mast.

"What is that?" I asked, not that any of us would know. "Is that something that's on every ship?" I didn't remember ever seeing one on the *Gem*.

"You know . . ." Erik said, ignoring my question. Maybe for once, I'd asked him something he didn't have an answer to. "There's still Savarah."

I thought back to the last time I'd seen her, arms around my brother, golden curls wild as she dangled over Bruhier. Then I thought about the tree monster, and the pile of firewood it had become at the base of the plateau. A fall like that . . . "I don't think we have to worry about her anymore." I glanced back at the griffin, who still sat at the edge of the clearing, and wondered if I was wrong about Savarah. If she'd been a monster wrapped in a beautiful package.

"No one saw her fall," Erik objected.

"Where else could she have gone? It's not like there was anywhere for her to hide on that ledge."

"I just—" Erik paused, pursing his lips. "There was something off about her, wasn't there? I wouldn't underestimate her, Frida."

I scoffed. "I wouldn't overestimate her." Things had been fine between us until we'd started talking about Savarah, and now the tension between us was pulled taut again. Time for a change of subject. "I think we should be more concerned with Luthair showing up and seeing us standing here with his men's blood on our hands."

"I would welcome him with open arms," Estrid declared, grinning wickedly.

Aria and Arun made their way back down the mast. Arun reached out to steady her as she descended, his hands on her hips, and I felt a pang of something like anger that I quickly shook off.

"Well?" I asked when they approached.

"The sheriu box is intact, which means she can fly," he said.

I glanced up at the blue box and wondered what, exactly, a sheriu box was, but now was not the time to ask.

"We just have to fix her sails and make sure she's structurally sound, and she'll get off the ground."

"What do you need to fix it?" Erik asked.

Arun turned to Aria. "There were sail repair kits on the supply deck with bone needles, thread, and patches." Just the mention of those supplies made my hand throb.

"I'm on it." Aria boarded the ship once more and disappeared into its innards.

"The rest is just manpower." Arun sounded confident, and I thought maybe we really would get off of this island.

"We should have plenty of that." Erik looked around at us and at the men on deck, still gathering bits of wood and ripped sail.

I was about to ask how long it would take when there was a loud squawking sound. A couple flocks of birds took flight from the nearby trees, their black bodies drawing circles around each other in the sky as they scrambled for . . . What?

The griffin stood, eyes lifted to the birds. She made a strange clicking noise in her throat.

Was it dinnertime?

Her wings stayed folded close to her body as she surveyed the disturbance.

"What—" I started but didn't finish, because then there was something else in the sky, a large, dark figure barely visible through the cloud of birds.

My first thought was a dreadwing, but then it burst through

the birds in an explosion of feathers, and I saw it was a creature like none I had seen before. Part human, part bird, all monster. Its body was grotesquely human, long limbs misshapen and grey, but leathery wings sprouted from its back with a wingspan wider than I was tall. Its humanoid face was all wrong, with a prominent brow, high cheekbones, and a flat nose. Thick, twisted horns sprouted from its forehead. Massive lower incisors reached up over its thin lips, which were stretched into a grotesque grin as it grabbed a bird out of the air and ripped its head off with its teeth. It roared, and dozens more appeared, scattering the birds, who dropped like stones to the ground.

Erik and Estrid shouted.

Arun readied an arrow in his bow, but the beasts flew past, a gruesome flock. And their trajectory had them heading straight for Barepost.

CHAPTER 20

I shouldn't have cared. I hated Barepost and most of the people in it. But it had been my home for the last three years. And I knew that they were woefully unprepared for an air attack, especially from creatures like those. They were always devastated by a dreadwing, who was slow and stupid. These creatures, whatever they were, clearly had some intelligence and, worst of all, cruel intentions.

"What were those?" Erik asked, echoing my own thoughts.

Surprisingly, it was Beru who answered. "Ur'gel."

I turned to him. "Ur'gel?" Seriously? I'd heard of them only in whispered stories of the Dark War, where they were described as weapons created by the gods on the side of Dag'-draath. They'd blended humans and animals and created something even worse than both. I remembered our father telling us that if we didn't get to sleep, the Drutha, a particularly terrible breed of ur'gel who was said to be practically invisible at night, would steal us away. It had been just a tale to scare us into behaving. It certainly hadn't been real. I wanted to declare it impossible but then thought of everything I'd seen over the last few years and realized I had no room to call anything impossible, not anymore.

"We must help your people." Beru headed away from the clearing and back the way we had come.

"They're not my people." But even as I said it, I realized it wasn't entirely true. I looked back at my brother and sister.

Estrid shrugged and turned to Erik.

He stood beside Arun, holding his bandaged arm close to his chest. "We can't abandon the people of Barepost. You three go, see if you can help. I would join you, but . . ."

"Erik, Arun, and I will stay," Aria declared with a stern look toward Erik, who was in no shape to climb or fight with his injured arm. "We'll get the ship in the air. You all just get back here safely, ready to fly." Even though she spoke to all of us, her eyes were on Beru.

What were they to each other?

Aria was so bright, so alive, while Beru was quiet and brooding, the darkness to her light. And if he didn't stop staring at the star beside my eye, I would shove him down the mountainside.

"Are you sure?" Estrid asked Erik.

He nodded, and I was glad for it.

For once, it would be up to us to do the hard work, and it would be Erik anxiously awaiting our return.

Beru, Estrid, and I turned and ran down the wooded path, coming quickly back to the abandoned guard station which was still spitting black smoke into the night sky. We ignored the fire and the fallen bodies and ran through the gate, back into the woods, and toward the cliff's edge where we had come up. From here, I could see the watch fires burning in Barepost, and though I couldn't see much other than dark forms against the night sky, I could hear the terrified screams of the people in the town, and the clash of metal on metal as the guards engaged with the bird-men.

I hoped Gerves and Grissall had taken cover. I hoped Harbin

was still on the *Gem*, somewhere far away from here. I remembered how the ur'gel had snapped that bird's neck and even
hoped Aysche and Luthair were hidden away safely in the house
on the ridge. No one deserved to meet that kind of end.

"It's going to take forever to get down," Estrid said even as
Beru was already lowering himself over the edge and dropping
to the ledge below.

She was right. By the time we got down there, it would practically be morning and Barepost would be long destroyed by
those monsters. Just as I was trying to invent a quicker way
down, and wondering if it would be quicker to go through the
path in the mine, there was a sound behind me like the call of a
large bird.

I turned in time to see a whole herd of griffins burst
through the trees, led by the one who had been watching us
by the airship, recognizable by the white band around her
eyes. They were running with their wings spread, their front
feet nearly coming off the ground as they prepared to take
flight.

Beru let go, dropping the few yards to the ledge below.

Estrid dove to the side to get out of their way.

But not me.

Because what quicker way down the cliff was there than
flying? When the griffins were nearly on top of me, I took two
running steps and then leapt, the griffin beside me, her wing
nearly brushing against me.

For a terrifying moment, I was falling, certain that I would
end up like the tree monster or Savarah, in pieces on the forest
floor. I heard Estrid call my name, saw Beru reach for me as I
fell past him, and then my grasping hands found fur and skin
and powerful muscle, and I held on tight, my fingers wrapping
around the fur coating the griffin's wide, muscled back. Even as
she wheeled and bucked, I held on tight, finally managing to
pull myself onto her back, tucking my knees behind her wing

joints and squeezing. It was like riding a horse, I told myself. A giant, flesh-eating, flying horse.

After her initial protest, the griffin didn't seem to mind having a passenger. She stopped diving and leveled out.

One of her friends drew up beside us, its eyes fixed on me, its head cocked to the side as it tried to figure out what this strange creature was.

I laughed and straightened up, slowly spreading my arms and tilting my face to the sky. How was it that, in such a terrible world, there could be such beautiful moments and such magnificent creatures?

When my mother had left, my father tried to convince me of that. I'd been young, but not so young that it hadn't hurt. Not so young that I hadn't felt the sting of shame and guilt, the burn of the betrayal by a world that had, until then, been kind to me. He had taken me out to the hills where we spied on a family of young forest cats playing beneath the canopy of leaves. We'd hiked to the fields during the first snow and watched the winter flowers burst to life, blue and silver against the white powder. We'd lain on soft grass beneath black skies and watched the stars wink to life, pinpricks in the dark canopy.

But that doubt had always been there, that belief that this world was, on its inside, a terrible place, full of anger and betrayal and abandonment. That its beauty was just a cover, that something horrible was always waiting beneath it. Now, though, as the griffin rose into the sky, I thought that maybe I finally understood what my father was trying to tell me. That the darkness didn't exist beneath the beauty, but that the beauty existed in spite of the darkness, and that it all depended on my perception. It all depended on what I chose to see.

The griffin's powerful muscles flexed beneath me, her wings beating in long, steady strokes to keep us aloft. We were high above Bruhier now, and soon we were inside the veil, that everpresent layer of clouds. Moisture gathered on my skin, and I couldn't see. I felt the panic tightening my throat, but then we were on the other side, the veil below us. Far away to the north, I saw lights of a distant town on a plateau, high above the dangers of the monsters below. Lamruil, I thought, the elven city. Overhead, the stars shone down on us, and I wondered what my ancestors thought of me now.

I leaned forward, putting my hands on the beast's neck. "Take us down." I applied gentle, downward pressure to her shoulders. I didn't know if she would understand or if she would even let me go, but eventually she turned and tucked her wings in a bit so that we began to descend.

As Barepost came back into view, so did the horror there. Families fled from burning houses just to be snatched up by flying ur'gel. The ur'gel would then lift them high into the sky and drop them, leaving a trail of broken bodies littering the ground in their wake. For a moment, I lamented not having Arun and his bow with us, but then the griffin dove. My heart leapt into my throat, and I held on tight as she crashed into an ur'gel, tearing at it with teeth and claws. The ur'gel bellowed in surprise, scratching at the griffin with its claw-like fingernails. I took out my ax and, as the griffin shifted, swung it at the ur'gel's throat, spraying all of us with black blood. It dropped out of the sky without another sound.

Over and over we did this, the griffin and I, attacking from above, a strategy I never in my life would have come up with. I didn't know where the rest of her herd was, or Estrid and Beru. I didn't know why she was helping me. Nothing made sense, but I fought on, dispatching ur'gel after ur'gel until we were both covered in their thick black blood. There was no time to stop or think or question.

We had just sent one more to its death when something slammed into us, nearly knocking me from my perch. The griffin squawked and spun to face her attacker.

There was no one there. Just the inky blackness of the sky.

Below us, someone screamed, but before we could move, there was another blow, this time to our other side. When I looked, I saw it. The ur'gel latched onto the griffin's wing.

The griffin screamed, trying to get her claws up to strike at the monster.

I should have helped, should have taken an ax to the beast's head, but I was too busy holding on, my injured hand throbbing. We were falling, spiraling out of control through the air as the griffin lost the use of her wing. The ur'gel was relentless, holding on and bellowing with what I thought could only be joy.

The ground rushed up at us. Holding on with my legs and one hand, I grabbed my ax, but it was too far away for me to hit. So, I took a deep breath, shutting out the screams in my ears and the wind in my face and the panic in my gut, and aimed. We spun once, caught the wind, and I threw the ax. For a second, I saw Jesper, the ax between his eyes, but then it was the ur'gel again, its eyes lifeless as it released the wing.

But the damage was done. The griffin's wing was destroyed, torn to shreds like the sails on Arun's ship.

We were still falling, but slower now as the griffin worked to compensate for the lost wing. I knew that I was weighing her down, so when we were close enough, I jumped from her back. She landed with a thump and collapsed to the ground. I put a hand on her head.

"You did good," I told her, and she closed her eyes.

There was no time to drag her to safety, no time to mourn. We had landed right in the middle of Barepost. Many of the ur'gel had taken to the ground now, busting down doors and dragging people outside, mauling them in the street. I found the ur'gel that had attacked us and pulled my ax from its head, wiping the black blood on its thick grey hide. We were close to the Gold Mine, and when I heard a shout from inside, I darted away, weaving through the panicked residents of Barepost and into the pub's open door.

The interior was dark, but I paused, listening, in the doorway. For a moment, I heard nothing but my heart pounding, and then there was a crash from the kitchen.

"Leave us alone!" Grissall's tiny voice shouted.

I leapt over the bar and banged through the swinging door to the kitchen beyond. Four sets of eyes met mine—two human and two something else. Grissall and Gerves were huddled in the back corner, Grissall wielding a shining knife and Gerves with nothing more than his bare fists. I remembered that he'd given my brother his only weapon, the galestone pistol that had saved our lives when we'd encountered the tree monster.

Two ur'gel bore down on them, but their attention had thankfully shifted to me. One of the ur'gel looked much like the first one we'd seen up by the airship, but the second was something else, something *other*. Instead of leathery bat wings, he had feathered wings that, even though they were folded against his back, rose high above his head in black arches. Its face was more human than the others, with average features topped with dark eyebrows and long, stringy hair. But its hands were gruesomely large, the fingers extended into long claws, and its legs and feet strangely feline.

"Are you ready to meet Dag'draath, human?" it asked in a strange, hissing voice that sent shivers down my spine.

I hadn't known that ur'gel had the power of speech.

I drew my sword and my ax, spinning them once around my hands. "You're mistaken," I said. "I'm not human. I'm D'ahvol."

"It is all the same to us."

It attacked, swiping with its long claws.

I jumped back out of the way as the other one grabbed for my arm. I knocked its hand away and brought my ax down, slicing through thick skin and bone. Its hand fell the floor.

Grissall screamed.

The ur'gel bellowed, turning to her as if realizing she was the easier target. It reached for her with its good hand, and I drove my sword through its back just before it made contact. But it came at the cost of ignoring the other ur'gel, the bigger threat to me.

The second ur'gel, the only one still alive, took advantage of my distraction to drive its claws into the back of my shoulder. I wasn't able to stop the scream rising up in my throat. Looking down, I saw one of its claws poking all the way through my shoulder, coming through the front, my own blood staining my shirt red.

"Frida!" shrieked Grissall, and before I could stop her, she'd thrown herself at the monster.

"No!" Gerves cried, but he was too late.

Grissall, small and insubstantial as she was, knocked the ur'gel back. It ripped its claws from my shoulder, the pain turning my vision black for a moment, and wrapped her in a gruesome hug.

I saw it coming, imagined him ripping her in two right there in front of her father. I saw how it would damage Gerves, how he would blame me, how it would all be my fault. I groped for my weapon, tried to stand, fell again. And then the ur'gel dropped Grissall, and we all froze as she tumbled to the floor and scooted away, back to Gerves's arms. There was a knife buried in the monster's neck. Its eyes were wide with shock as it fell, gave one last gasp, and grew still.

"Onen save me," Grissall gasped, staring at the bodies on the floor, at the blood seeping from my wound.

"No," I said, "you saved us."

Except for the hole in my shoulder, the wounds in my back were mostly superficial. Even the one in my shoulder had gone through cleanly, not tearing anything that wouldn't heal.

Grissall cleaned the wounds with alcohol while I gritted my teeth against the pain of her ministrations, and then bound the shoulder with clean rags from the bar. It was my left shoulder, my ax-wielding side, the same side with the injured hand. I was glad that it seemed like most of the fighting was over, at least for now.

"This will have to do." she said. "You said you have a healer?"

"There's a healer waiting for me. We're leaving."

"Luthair let you go?" Gerves asked. He stood at the door, watching the battle rage in the street beyond.

"No. But it's time for us to leave."

He turned his eyes away briefly, finding mine. "Good for you. Good for all of you."

"Come with me."

Grissall looked at her father, then at the floor. "I couldn't."

"No," Gerves said, "I couldn't. But you can, if you wanted to. Perhaps it is for the best. There aren't many chances to leave Barepost. And you have proven that you can handle yourself."

"Leaving Barepost would mean leaving you." Grissall looked between her father and me.

"Well, you would always know where to find me when you wanted to come back home."

I thought of Haklang betraying Luthair so that we would take Xalph away from here. I thought of my own father back in Bor'sur, of his last words to me before we'd boarded the *Sea Spider*.

"Go," he'd said. "Have your adventures. Make your fortunes. Find your fame. I'll be here when you are ready to return."

Before Grissall could answer, Gerves stepped back from the door just as it burst open.

Alarmed, I turned, pain shooting down my arm, but it was just Estrid followed by Beru, both of them looking tattered and windblown and splattered with black blood.

"I thought I'd find you here," Estrid said breathlessly. "Come on, you have to see this."

CHAPTER 21

E strid was right. If I hadn't seen it with my own eyes, I never would have believed it. It wasn't just griffins and humans fighting the ur'gel now, but all types of cliff monsters had joined in the fray. They were chasing each other through the streets and the sky in a chaos of wings and teeth and claws.

"What happened?"

A dreadwing and an ur'gel collided in an explosion of feathers overhead that sent us staggering away.

"After you did maybe the stupidest thing I have ever seen you do—and there have been a lot of stupid things, so that's not an easy accomplishment—there was a mass exodus from the mountaintop. All kinds of monsters you've never even seen were swarming down the cliff to hunt the ur'gel. So"— she said with a shrug, motioning to Beru—"we hitched a ride."

"On what?"

Estrid grimaced. "Well, I . . . I rode a dreadwing."

"You did what?" I hissed. "And you called me stupid? It could have carried you off and fed it to its babies."

"So could the griffin." Strangely, Estrid fought to keep a smile off of her face. "Besides, it wasn't that bad."

"Wasn't that—" I stopped and turned on Beru. "And what did you ride?"

"Some sort of long-necked demon bird," he said, and it was as close as I'd ever heard him come to making a joke.

That was when an ur'gel fell from the sky. One of its wings was ripped, but that didn't stop it from lunging at us. Beru was closest. With two strikes of his sword, he cut the monster down. When it fell, we readied ourselves for more but were surprised to find it fairly quiet.

I looked up and saw several dark figures disappearing into the veil, followed by a colorful array of different cliff monsters, all in different sizes and shapes.

After a few moments of quiet, Gerves emerged from the pub, Grissall peeking over his shoulder. "Is that it? Are they gone?"

"I think so." There were bodies everywhere, human and ur'gel and monster alike. And there, a few yards away, the griffin with the white band around her eyes sat watching us, her broken wing hanging limply at her side, the other one tucked against her back. She had black ur'gel blood on her beak and claws, but she looked as stoic and disinterested as ever.

I left Beru and Estrid talking about how to get back up the mountain and approached the griffin, stopping an arm's length away. I reached a hand toward her beak, knowing that with a snap of her powerful jaws, I'd be left mangled for the rest of my life. But I didn't think she would do that. I felt that we had bonded during that battle.

"Will you let me help you?"

She stared back with blank eyes. "We can mend your wing, get you back in the air again."

Though I was sure she had no idea what I said, perhaps it was my tone of voice that inspired her to dip her head into my waiting hand.

Her beak was hard, like stone, but the feathers on her face were soft and fluffy, like those of a newborn chick. I ran my fingers up between her eyes and scratched behind her head. Her tail twitched, but she made no other movement.

But then her back went stiff, and her head snapped up. She twisted her long neck around, and the rest of her body followed as she nudged me to the side with her hip. She was making that strange clicking noise in her throat that I decided was a growl.

I peeked around her, and that was when I saw what—or who—had her on edge. Who she was protecting me from.

Luthair stood in the otherwise empty alley, completely alone without a black-clad guard in sight. He was dressed all in black, though, from his boots to his tunic. His cloak was bright red, clasped at the neck with a golden brooch. The belt across his chest didn't hold a sword, but instead bags of coin. He didn't seem intimidated by the griffin but was looking past her, to me. There was a look on his face that I'd never seen before—it was open, vulnerable, hurt—things I didn't know he could feel. He knew, then, that we'd come from the plateau, that we'd helped Arun and the others escape. That I'd been lying to him all along.

He looked behind me at Estrid, then to Beru, then back at me. "If you are here and your brother is not, does it mean you have given my offer some thought?"

"What offer?" Estrid asked.

"I'm only here to help the town," I said, ignoring Estrid, not wanting to answer her question or even think about his offer of marriage.

"The town does not need you anymore."

I laughed. "There are ur'gel attacking Barepost, and you say that now you don't need us? Why are they here? What are they looking for?"

"Maybe for you," Beru said quietly behind me.

I turned, my brow furrowed, not sure who he could be talking about, but certainly not me.

"Barepost is safe." Luthair drew our attention back to him. "It's time to decide. Will it be you or Erik?"

"We're leaving," I said, a hand on the griffin's back. "All of us."

She opened her mouth and squawked at him, showing him the rows of teeth.

"You're not." There was no hint of doubt in his voice. He believed his control over us to be complete. "I don't give you permission, and there is no other way off this island." He didn't know, then, that we'd already found the airship. That though it had been under guard and destroyed, we'd still found it and were working on fixing it even now, as he gloated, thinking we were stuck here at his mercy. "You have one hour to decide—you or Erik. I have a feeling I know what your answer will be." He paused. "I'll have Missus prepare your room."

He turned and walked away.

I lunged, but Estrid caught my arm. "What is he talking about?"

"He's talking about me marrying him. Either I marry him or he sentences Erik to life in the mines in Arun's place." I looked at Luthair's retreating back, then again at Estrid. "I don't see why you care. Either way, you're free to go."

She shoved me back.

The griffin turned her head to glare at Estrid.

"Don't even think about it," she growled at the griffin, who promptly sat and began scratching her own back with her beak.

"Traitor," I grumbled.

"You don't see why I care that one of my siblings could be lost to me forever? You don't think this is a choice that you should have involved Erik and me in?"

"It doesn't matter." I took a step back. "We're going to leave on the airship as soon as it's ready to go."

She ignored me. "First you go and accept this job against Erik's wishes. Then you enter into a bargain with an elf who isn't even there. And now I find out that this whole time, you've been bargaining with Luthair too."

"I'm not—" I stopped and spun around, leaning against a wall to collect myself. She was always like this. She always had to have all the facts, to know exactly what was going on, to be in complete control. How could I convince her that everything I did, I did for them? For us? "We can't stay here forever." I turned back to her and lowered my voice. "We have to find a way out of here, a way home. All of us. No one is staying here."

Estrid scoffed, but before she could say more, I turned to Beru, who had been staying out of the conversation. "What did you mean earlier? About the ur'gel looking for me? And why are you always staring at me?"

"Not at you, at the mark beside your eye." He looked surprised but didn't deny it. "You don't know what it is?" he asked. "The star?"

"It's a blessing from my ancestors," I answered.

"Yes, in a way. It is said that when the Creator made the old gods—Time, Power, Earth, and Death—that he gave them the ability to create new gods in their image. Death and Power created Dag'draath, who very quickly became a blight upon this world. To combat him, Time and Earth sent us Onen Suun. The Creator, who saw the destruction that Dag'draath would wreak, blessed Onen Suun with a kiss on the temple, marking him forever as one of his own, as a creature of the Light who would have the power to defeat the Dark."

Beru reached up and touched the mark. "The kiss took on the shape of a star and was to be passed on to all of his descendants. You, Frida Svand, are perhaps a Svand but only in name. You are Onen Suun's only remaining heir."

"That's impossible."

Beside me, Estrid stood stunned and silent, a rarity for her.

"There's more. I was Onen Suun's most trusted general."

I laughed, but when no one else did, I stopped. "But that would make you hundreds of years old."

"Just before the end of the Dark War, I'd been captured by Dag'draath, and when Onen Suun imprisoned Dag'draath's men in the Barren Wastes, I was on the wrong side of the enchantment, doomed to spend eternity in the darkness. That is how I am still alive. But Aria is a dreamwalker."

A dreamwalker? I looked at Estrid.

She didn't look at me.

Did Erik know what that meant?

Beru continued without giving us a chance to ask questions. "She visited me in the Barren Wastes and pulled me from that place. And when she did, she made a crack in the prison walls."

"The ur'gel,"

"Yes. They're fleeing into the world with the darkness that seeps from the crack. The crack will continue to grow, and the creatures will only get worse—darker and more dangerous— until Dag'draath himself is unleashed once more upon Iynia."

"How do we stop it?"

"You are the key," he said. "As Onen Suun's heir, you are the only one able to close the prison again. To fix the mistake that Aria and I made. To save the world."

CHAPTER 22

I did not want to save the world.

That was not to say that I did not want the world to be saved, but I certainly did not want it to be my responsibility. I wanted to save myself and my siblings, get us off this blasted island, and go home.

I stared at Beru, studying his face. His *200-year-old* face. There were no wrinkles, no grey strands of hair, nothing to indicate he was any older than maybe thirty. Nothing to indicate he had stood beside Onen Suun or faced down Dag'draath's armies. Things that were—to me and nearly everyone else alive —mere stories, things that happened so long ago that they hardly seemed real anymore. It was ridiculous to think that I was somehow connected to those old stories. That I was some key to saving the world.

A blessing from my ancestors. A kiss from the Creator, a mark of Onen Suun. Perhaps one and the same, if Beru were to be believed. I wondered if my father knew about my mother's heritage, that she was descended from gods. Was that how he'd known what the mark was, or was it a lucky guess? Did it have something to do with her departure, this connection to the gods and the growing darkness in the Barren Wastes?

I felt Estrid watching me before I even turned to look at her. She'd known my mother, remembered her better than I did.

"Was my mother marked? Did she have?" I waved a hand beside my eye.

Estrid shook her head. "That didn't even show up until after she left."

I was still thinking, trying to come up with questions to ask, when Aria appeared behind Beru. He turned and blinked in surprise. "What are you doing here?"

"I'm here to fetch you." Her face looked flushed like she'd run here. "We saw the ur'gel leave. The ship is ready. Arun wants to go before they come back."

It seemed like a solid plan to me.

But Estrid grabbed my arm before I could follow Beru and Aria. "Erik will not go."

"What are you talking about?"

"You must know this. He won't be on that ship when it takes off. Not unless Luthair releases him of his debt."

"Not even Erik is that stubborn." He had to know I wouldn't leave him. He had to know I would give myself up for him, no matter what Beru said.

"He might have helped put that airship back together, but I never heard him agree to go. He owes Luthair—even if it was our fault—and he's going to repay that debt. You don't know him like I do."

The words stung, especially considering what I'd learned today. That I was a Svand but only in name. Whether or not it was true, it made me feel even more distant from Erik and Estrid. I looked past Estrid to where Aria and Beru were waiting for us at the corner.

They thought I was supposed to save the world. Maybe Erik

would believe it too. Maybe that would be enough to convince him to get onto the airship. There was an urgency to my desire to get out of Barepost that I hadn't felt before, not truly. It was like our carefully constructed world was imploding, and I was ready to go along with the ridiculous lie if it got us away from here.

"I didn't mean it like that." Estrid put a hand on my shoulder as if to comfort me.

I shook her off. "I know, I just—I think I can convince him. Just trust me, this once."

Estrid looked taken aback, ready to argue again.

A small voice called out. "Frida."

I turned.

Grissall stood a few yards away, the injured griffin at her side and a brown bag on her back. "I'm going with you. If that's okay."

Gerves stood beyond them, in the door to the pub.

"Yes. Yes, I mean . . ." I looked past her to Gerves.

He raised a hand in farewell and disappeared inside the pub.

"I mean, of course." I waved her closer, and she shuffled forward shyly. I was glad she was there, but for purely selfish reasons. Glad that Estrid wouldn't fight with me in front of her. Glad that I could use her as another excuse to get us out of Barepost.

The griffin trailed after her.

"You too?"

The animal nudged me with her feathered head.

I scratched behind its ears. Her wing still drooped. I studied it, trying to figure out what to do.

Estrid brought a length of rope. "Here. Bind the wing. She'll climb up with us."

The griffin sat still as I wrapped the rope around her, binding her injured wing to her body so that it wouldn't drag along the ground or get caught up in her feet. When I was practically beneath her, she reached down and nipped at my hair. At first I was startled, but then I realized it was an affectionate gesture, maybe even teasing.

Done, I stepped back and surveyed my work. She nibbled at the rope, then stopped, seeming to declare it suitable, at least for now.

"You'll need a name."

She looked over at me. Her dark eyes reflected the morning sun that peeked through the clouds behind me. It looked like hundreds of stars sparkling against the night sky.

Look up, my star.

"Stiarna." It was the Ahvoli word for star, and it seemed to fit her perfectly, just as it had once fit me.

"Frida!" Estrid shouted back to me. "Your hour is almost up. We don't want someone to come looking for you. Let's go."

I patted Stiarna on the side. "Come on. We're not done yet."

Estrid led the way back through Barepost, Stiarna and I bringing up the rear. We raced down alleyways and crept across intersections. The town was still reeling from the attack, and hardly anyone noticed us, even with a griffin trailing us. Many people were mourning, their wails shaking me to my core. Others were quietly cleaning or repairing doors or putting out smoldering fires. No one smiled or called to anyone else. It made me hate Luthair even more, that he was worried about himself and how to best control me at a time like this, when his people truly needed him.

In a way, though, I was glad for his selfishness, because it meant he wasn't out helping the townsfolk. Instead, he was squirreled away in his house on the ridge waiting for me. Which was just fine. He would be waiting a long time, and that way, he wouldn't see us leaving.

We were nearly to the gate when we paused to regroup.

"How do we do this?" Estrid asked.

I barely had time to appreciate that she was really asking me when Beru answered. "We take them by surprise. They've left the gate practically unguarded. The odds are in our favor."

I was just considering the strangeness of that fact—that things were actually going our way—when a hand clapped down on my shoulder.

I whirled around and came face to face with Aysche, or the wraith that had once been her. She looked awful. The black kohl she used to line her eyes was smudged and streaked, looking more like war paint than a beauty tool. But it wasn't just the kohl that coated her hands and face and pretty pink dress. The thick black liquid was familiar—ur'gel blood.

"Wow." I looked her up and down as she'd done to me so many times before. How she still managed to look indignant was beyond me.

"Was this you?"

"What?"

"Was this you? Some petty, D'ahvol revenge plot?"

"Aysche?" Estrid appeared over my shoulder.

From beneath her skirts, Aysche drew a small knife. Most of the women in Barepost chose to carry them instead of real weapons that could actually be useful against a monster, so that wasn't surprising. What was surprising was that she waved it in my face.

I didn't even draw my blades. "You think that I brought ur'gel from the Blasted Lands and set them on Barepost to get back at you?" She and her uncle really were exactly alike, both of them thinking that the world revolved around them.

"Ur'gel?" I could tell that at first, she wanted to laugh, but then she saw the truth in what I said. That these hadn't been ordinary Bruhier monsters. But there was no reasoning with her. She shook her head, as if shaking off the logic, and waved her knife at me again. "I'll kill you for this."

I didn't think that was likely. She wanted to. That was obvious. She needed somewhere to place the blame that wasn't on herself or on her uncle. But that knife and her wielding skills would do little against me. This was the girl who had hidden behind as many people as possible when the fight broke out on the *Gem*. Who had lashed out at me with words but never with fists. I realized then, for maybe the first time, that she was just a scared, weak little girl living in a dangerous place. The only way she knew how to protect herself was to climb on the shoulders of those she could manipulate. Anyone else, anyone who defied her, like me, scared her.

Estrid shrugged and turned back to Aria and Beru.

"No, you won't." I turned away, Stiarna at my side.

"You will pay for this," Aysche shouted at my back. "Wicked D'ahvol. I curse you!"

Her voice faded as I walked away and didn't look back.

Surprisingly, it was Aria who got us through the gate. While Beru and Estrid were still arguing about the best strategy to fight our way out, Aria walked right up to the gate master and requested that he give us passage.

"Your funeral," he said, opening a small door through the guardhouse and giving us and Stiarna a wide berth as we exited. I guessed he had more to worry about now than the Svands.

"You could have gotten hurt or arrested," Beru grumbled when the door slammed behind us, the iron lock sliding into place.

Aria shrugged. "Sometimes warriors see only the fight. Don't forget that there are often easier ways. Ways that don't actually involve bloodshed."

Beru harrumphed, reminding me of Erik in that moment.

Laughing, Estrid thumped him on the back. "Sure, but they're a lot less fun."

The climb up the cliff was quicker this time, with Stiarna leading us up hidden, twisting paths. There were still some difficult passages, ones that would have been easier to traverse with wings or claws, some that even Stiarna stumbled a bit on without the use of her wings. Without the proper climbing gear,

I kept close to Grissall, who was ill-equipped for the difficult climb or anything that required much physical effort, really.

She and I had never really been friends, even though we lived beneath the same roof. For the first few months, she refused to speak to me, and when she did work up the nerve to do that, she kept her eyes on the ground, as if by looking at me, she would catch the disease that made me a D'ahvol. Eventually, after deciding that I would not, in fact, kill her for fun, she loosened up but still only spoke to me for practical matters—to take my order or to deliver my washing. I didn't dislike her, but I certainly didn't have any use for her. It would be interesting having her along now.

"Don't put your foot there," I told her as we crossed a narrow, natural stone bridge.

She picked her foot up just as the rock below it crumbled, leaving a small gap. The look she shot me told me she regretted ever coming along.

"It's fine, don't panic. Just be careful."

"As if I'm not."

I nearly laughed at her defiance. Perhaps saving my life had given her the confidence she needed to contend with me. "Barepost careful and climbing-a-cliff careful are two totally different things."

It was then, as she looked back at me to make some scathing retort, that she slipped. I reached for her, but she was already too far away, only one person able to be on the bridge at a time. She slid, her boots scraping the cliffside, her hands grasping for something, anything to hold.

Then a hooked beak snagged in the collar of her shirt.

Grissall yelped as she was jerked backward into the air and deposited none-too-gently on the other side of the path.

Stiarna released her shirt and blinked down at her.

"Th-thanks," Grissall stuttered.

A small, nervous laugh bubbled up in my throat as Stiarna nipped at Grissall's curly hair and then turned away, following the path up the mountain with careful steps, as if showing Grissall exactly where to put her feet. No one waited for me, but I made it across fine and scrambled after them.

We were nearly at the top, passing by the entrance to some small cave, when I heard a small growl from within. I stopped and peered in, and found myself face-to-face with a long snout and two large, protruding fangs.

I froze and held my breath as the cave dragon sniffed, its nose twitching. It took one step forward, and I took one back, my heel slipping off the ledge.

It came into the light, and I saw the black blood coating its fur, and a red, open wound on its neck. Behind it, I heard the growl of another creature.

"Me too," I said, my voice a whisper.

It sniffed again, its tongue darting out, and then it withdrew back into the cave.

"Frida!" Estrid shouted from somewhere up ahead. "Let's go!"

I slid sideways, not turning my back on the cave until I was past it. It may not have attacked me then, but I still didn't trust its claws.

We reached the top of the plateau without further incident and followed the path through the woods, past the gate, and toward the clearing where the *Iron Duchess* waited. But as we grew closer, our pace slowed.

Estrid dropped back beside me. "Something feels wrong."

"I know." I felt it too. There was a stillness in the air, an unnatural silence. Nothing rustled, nothing moved. There was no sound from the men we'd left at the airship.

We came across the first body a few yards into the woods. A miner whose name I didn't know, his throat slit from ear to ear. Dozens of boot prints were pressed into the dirt and leaves around him. We followed the path of broken branches and muddy ground to the next body. He lay on his belly, white hair soaked red with blood. I rolled him over.

"Bertol," I breathed.

His eyes were still open, blue-grey and glassy.

"Was this the ur'gel?" Grissall asked.

I bent down, examining the wounds in Bertol's stomach and chest. "No," I answered, my fingers brushing another bootprint. "Definitely not."

I felt sick, seeing Bertol like this, knowing that he dreamed of being outside the mines, that he longed to feel rain on his face.

Beside me, Estrid looked down at the body, her face stricken. "Erik."

"Estrid, wait," I started, but she was already gone.

She wasn't following any trail or trying to be quiet.

The rest of us ran after her, pushing aside branches and weaving around trees and fallen logs.

Stiarna was the fastest of us, easily pulling into the lead. But then we all skidded to a stop as we came into the clearing where the airship sat, with repaired railings and patched sails. On the deck, Xalph and Arun stood surrounded by six guards, while on the ground, another six held Erik, his hands bound in front of him. There was no one else from the mines in sight.

Except for Luthair.

His face was closed again. Gone was the vulnerability and the pain I'd seen in Barepost. He was smug again, knowing that he'd won. He stood very close to Erik, close enough that Erik could easily have gotten his hands around the governor's neck. If he wanted to. But Erik wouldn't do that. Estrid was right. He wouldn't do anything to compromise his honor, including board an airship to leave Barepost without being released from his life-debt.

Luthair grinned, keeping one hand on the hilt of the

longsword sheathed at his hip, a sword I'd never, not once, seen him draw. "Surprised?"

I wouldn't give him the pleasure of saying yes, of asking how he'd gotten up here so quickly and with so many men.

"I know Bruhier and this plateau better than anyone." He pointed at Stiarna, who stood beside me, her head low to the ground, her eyes on Luthair. "Even better than your new pet."

Stiarna snapped her beak and made the clicking growl sound in her throat.

"Let them go."

He looked over at Erik, then behind him at Arun and Xalph. Did he realize who Xalph was? Would Haklang be punished? Or had it been so long that he'd forgotten about his illegitimate nephew? "I know you thought you could get away without making a choice." He turned back to me. "You probably thought I was foolish, giving you the chance to get away. Really, I just needed you to think you had an hour, to think you could take your time returning, so that I could get here first."

"Why are you here?" I asked, growing tired of his gloating.

"I'm here to force your hand, of course."

"What are you talking about?" Estrid spat at him.

"Your brother can go, and Estrid, you can go with him, if Arun Phina goes back to the mines and if your sister agrees to marry me." He held out his hands in front of him, palms up, innocent, as if offering a gift. "Or, you"—he pointed at me—"and you"—his finger shifted to Estrid—"can go with the elf, but Erik will spend the rest of his life in the mines. Though we'll have to gather a new group for him, of course."

"Bastard!" Estrid lunged.

Beru grabbed her.

Stiarna growled and began to pace.

I put a hand on her shoulder, and she became frightfully still.

"Is that really what you want?" I asked. "For your bride to be a prisoner?"

He shrugged, unconcerned. "I want you to do what's right for your family. I'll do what's right for Barepost."

As if either of those options were valid. But there was something else, something I'd never tried before. Something that occurred to me as I watched him shift his grip on the hilt of his sword while I considered the matter of Erik's blasted honor. While Luthair wasn't particularly honorable, he was certainly prideful, hopefully to a fault.

I took two steps forward, away from Estrid and the others and toward Luthair. I pulled my sword from its sheath.

The men around Erik shifted, suddenly uncertain about where to focus their attention, but Luthair waved them away.

I lay the blade of the sword over my left wrist. "Stephan Luthair, Governor of Barepost. I challenge you to a duel."

Luthair tried to keep the grin on his face, but I saw his lips pucker in distaste, saw the twitch of an eyebrow in surprise. "What are the terms?"

"Winner takes all."

"Frida, no!" Erik and Estrid shouted at the same time.

"All?" Luthair asked, ignoring my siblings.

"If you win and I surrender, Erik, Estrid, and I all stay, all continue to do your bidding until you release Erik from his life-debt. If I win, all of us," I said, gesturing to everyone around him, "go free. With your permission."

Everyone gathered in the clearing went still, even his own men, holding their breath while Luthair considered the offer. "Those are your only terms?"

"Yes," I said with a nod, feeling even as I agreed that I'd fallen into some type of trap.

Finally, Luthair pulled his own sword from its place at his hip. It was shiny and smooth, obviously unused. He lay it across his own left wrist and looked at me. "Frida Svand, D'ahvol warrior and future bride of Barepost, I accept your challenge."

I sneered at him and spun my sword around my arm. I liked

a good fight, but never had I been quite so happy to face someone on the battlefield than I was at that moment. It was time to put a few dents on that pristine blade of his.

CHAPTER 24

Luthair removed his cloak and handed it off to one of his men before squaring off against me. His stance was strange and shaky, while I made sure mine was steady. I watched his eyes instead of his sword, and when he came at me, twisting from the outside to the inside and striking my sword, I knocked him away easily, parrying just a bit to get the feel of him before driving forward with a series of quick blows back and forth.

I could see his frustration building as he failed to get past my guard. It showed in his moves. He grabbed the sword with two hands and made a slice to the left, which I avoided, and another slice to the right, which I also dodged. When he came across as if to cut me in half, I dropped to my knees, his blade passing overhead, and knocked his sword aside with my own.

I stood with a growl, driving him back until he was out of reach and I could regain my stance. He tried another overhead swing—a bad idea since it put him off balance—and I met it with my own sword. That was how it went for some time, our blades crashing together over and over as I took the defensive, not giving an inch. Finally, I spun low, going to the ground and kicking his knee. He yelped and stabbed at me, but I was already gone, dancing away on light feet.

"You remember your terms, right?" Luthair said a little breathlessly, his sword drooping slightly as he favored his left knee.

I nodded, smiling as my heart raced. The battle fever raged through my blood. I was done talking. I wanted to keep going.

"You said nothing about who could fight."

"Who?" I straightened, dropping my sword to my side as Luthair flicked his fingers at his men.

Luckily, Arun was not as slow on the uptake as I was. I watched as he shoved Xalph to the side and grabbed a sword from a nearby guard's scabbard.

Xalph scrambled across the deck, doing his best to avoid feet and swords.

Arun plunged the sword into one of the guard's chests just as Erik, hands still bound, got the twine around one of Luthair's men's necks, pulling tight and backing away. The man's eyes bulged. Erik evaded other advances, never loosening his grip, not until the man went slack in his arms and he let him fall to the ground.

Estrid, Beru, and Aria ran into the fray then, swords swinging. Even Stiarna pounced on a black-clad guard, holding him down with one of her front claws and ripping out his throat with her powerful beak. I wondered then if jumping onto her back had been an act of bravery or of insanity. Perhaps a bit of both.

Grissall's small form ran past Stiarna's kill toward the ship, where she scooped up Xalph, who had been huddling against the railing, and dove into the crew's quarters near the front of the ship, slamming the door.

Taking advantage of my distraction, Luthair leveled his blade at my throat.

I turned to him, eyes narrowed, ready to call him a liar and a cheater, but before I could get a word out, he brought a boot up and kicked me in the gut. I flew back, landing on my back. All the wind rushed out of me. I'd lost track of my sword in the fall, and I rolled, fingers groping through the leaves and dirt even as blackness encroached on my vision.

Not far away, I saw Beru and Aria fighting back to back. Instead of a sword, Aria had a staff with a metal-tipped blade on one end, the other end rounded. She wielded it with confidence and expertise. She said something to Beru, and he ducked as she swung the staff in a circle overhead, knocking down two of Luthair's men with the one move. Beru finished the other one with his sword.

Not far away, Erik and Estrid fought side by side. I'd grown up seeing them fight like this. They were like one brain in two bodies, each covering for the other's weakness. No one would be able to defeat them, not when they were together.

I rolled the other way, still searching for my sword.

On the deck of the *Duchess*, Arun had found a bow from somewhere and was using it in both close combat and to pick off Luthair's men from far away. When he had to, he used it like a staff of his own, knocking aside swords and burying arrows in men's necks with his bare hands.

Just when my fingers brushed metal, hands grabbed my ankles and pulled me backward, rolling me onto my back. Luthair loomed over me, putting a boot to my chest and pressing down so my lungs wouldn't fill. He held his sword, which, while still clean, now at least had a fair number of dings in the blade.

"Any last words?" he asked, looking down his long nose at me.

"If you fight dirty," I gasped, "you should always watch your back."

Stiarna's tail wrapped around his middle and lifted him off

the ground. He flailed, his sword falling beside me. I rolled as Stiarna slammed him down and then shook him back and forth, dragging him through the dirt. When she released him, he finally looked as dirty and ragged as every other person in Barepost.

I was on my feet again. I ran up to him, driving my boot into his gut as he tried to stand. He flopped back down.

With both our swords gone, I drew my ax. Its wooden handle was warm in my hand, the etched runes of my name familiar to the touch. I hadn't drawn it before because I'd wanted to play by the rules. I'd wanted to win fairly. But nothing about this duel had been fair. He'd brought other people into it. He'd hurt my friends and my family, people whom I loved. He'd tried to control me, to take away my dreams and write a different ending to my story.

I gathered Luthair's tunic into my hands and drew him up to my face.

"Frida." He wasn't smiling any more. His eyes darted to something over my shoulder and I turned in time to see Estrid drive a sword through the back of a guard who had been coming to save the governor. There was no one to save him now.

"Do you remember my terms?" I asked him, pressing the blade of the ax close enough to his neck that I could shave the tiny whiskers growing there.

"Yes." He gulped, his throat pulsing against the blade. "Yes, I remember."

"Winner takes all."

"Frida—"

"Convince me not to kill you," I hissed, my blood boiling.

His eyes searched my face. Finally, he spoke. "I surrender." He held both of his hands up.

He was betting on my honor. I didn't have to stop. I didn't have to be honorable—he certainly wasn't. He'd said we were alike once. I could prove him right. It would be so easy to rid the world of Stephan Luthair, but then what? Would Aysche come into power? I remembered what he told me about Barepost, how it had been before he'd taken over. As much as I hated him, at least Luthair knew what it took to run Barepost, to keep it from falling into chaos. It needed a firm hand. He was the one who could get it back on its feet after the ur'gel attack.

I dropped him, stepping away.

"Frida, what are you doing?" Estrid asked.

There were no guards left. We stood in a sea of bodies—black-clad guards and escaped miners ringed by scaled dragons. Stiarna was beside Estrid, looking eager to finish what she started with Luthair. The rest—Erik, Arun, Beru, Aria, Xalph, and Grissall—were on the deck of the *Duchess*, watching.

"You don't get to make the rules if you don't follow them," I said to Luthair. "The people of Barepost need you, and maybe they even need to fear you, but you need to be fair. And just. And kind every now and then."

Luthair was nodding emphatically, his shoulders slumping with relief.

I took a step closer to him and tipped his chin up with the blade of my ax, just to remind him of where he stood. "If you don't . . . I will end you. I will end you and destroy Barepost." Barepost was his home, for better or worse, and I thought that maybe that would get his attention.

"I concede. I agree to your terms." He pushed to his feet, brushing the dirt from his clothes and limping away toward the gate.

I expected there was a hidden lift there somewhere that he'd taken up. I wondered how he would get down, but it really didn't concern me.

Estrid wrapped me into a hug.

Luthair turned back around. "The offer still stands. If you

ever find yourself back in Barepost. I'm used to getting what I want, and I want you, Svand. I never lose."

I almost laughed. Instead, I shook my head at him. "Well, you did today."

He hobbled away, disappearing into the trees, leaving us, as usual, to clean up his mess.

CHAPTER 25

Erik hissed through his teeth as Aria applied a balm to the burns on his arm.

"I can't believe you did this to yourself," Aria spoke without looking at him, her attention on the angry red skin. "You're likely to have permanent damage."

She had already tended the wounds in my shoulder and hand, so I had also been adequately scolded. She'd said the shoulder would likely be sore on and off for the rest of my life but that the hand would recover with a minimal scar. I didn't care about the scar as long as I could still hold an ax.

"It was that or die," Estrid said in Erik's defense.

The four of us were sitting on the deck of the *Iron Duchess*. On the ground below, Arun and Beru were gathering the bodies of the dead miners and guards. Aria finished tending Erik's arm and then left the three of us alone, disappearing into the crews' quarters to check on Grissall and Xalph.

When she was gone, I turned to Erik. He wasn't speaking to me and had barely looked me in the eye since Luthair had left. "Are you upset with me?"

He stood, pulling his shirt over his head. "It wasn't your debt to settle."

"It was." I looked to Estrid for support. She pressed her lips together and nodded, not meeting Erik's eyes. "Look, I know we don't talk about it, but Estrid and I got you into that mess. We took Luthair up on his offer because we couldn't stand to lose you. But we lost you anyway."

"You didn't—"

"We did," Estrid confirmed, finally speaking up. "And the only way to keep a small part of you was by serving Luthair with you."

"I won your freedom," I said. "I won *our* freedom."

He stalked to the gangplank to leave the ship but paused and looked back at us. "If only it were that easy."

Arun did not think the miners would appreciate being buried, so that afternoon, we burned the bodies in an elven-style funeral pyre, which was really very similar to an Ahvoli burning ceremony, just without the funeral boat. It was more and more obvious that even though the D'avhol and the elves didn't intermingle much, we still maintained a lot of their traditions. We were maybe not so different after all.

At Aria's insistence, we buried the guards' bodies, even though it put us staying on the plateau another night to finish the work. I slept, and when I woke to take the last shift, Arun was already there. We sat together on the deck of the ship, watching the dark tree line. Thankfully, Stiarna stalking through the woods was the only creature we saw.

When it was past midnight, I leaned back on the palms of my hands and looked up at the sky. The veil had lowered, which it did rarely. This plateau wasn't protected by the clouds like the rest were. But that night, I could see stars. The sky looked a lot like it did at home in Bor'sur.

"It's been so long since I've seen a cloudless sky," I said almost without meaning to. I didn't want him to think I felt sorry for myself, not after everything that we'd been through. Everything we'd survived.

"It's been so long since I've seen a sky at all."

I cut my eyes to him, ready to apologize.

He was smiling. He bumped my shoulder with his and pointed to one of the brighter stars nearest to Aupra, the white moon. "Inara is bright tonight. We should have good weather for flying tomorrow."

I patted the deck beneath me. "Is she safe to fly? Truly?"

"Truly?" He laughed. "Shame, because I was so planning on lying."

"Really?" I sat upright, watching his face.

He laughed again. "You flew on a griffin, and you're afraid of my *Duchess*?"

"Not afraid," I corrected him. "Just . . . cautious."

"Since when are you cautious?"

I scoffed at him but was secretly pleased that he knew me so well.

Arun leaned back on his hands beside me, our shoulders brushing. "So where will you go, now that you're finally free?"

"Beru wants to take me to a temple on another plateau. He says there's a Priestess of Light there who might be able to confirm if I'm 'the one.'" I emphasized the two words to try to show how ridiculous I thought it was.

But Arun, who knew only the basics of Beru's theory about me being the savior of the world, didn't laugh. Instead, he shrugged. "I think I know the place. I'll take you there. I have nowhere else to be."

"Don't you want to go home?" I asked, thinking of Tsarra Trisfina and her family, and the mysterious Savarah. Thinking that it would be nice to see Lamruil, and it would delay any interrogation by a priestess who would try to figure out my identity before even I was sure.

"Eventually."

"Am I your next lost cause?" I was only half-joking.

Arun smirked. "You're not lost, Frida Svand. If anything, you're the one who showed me the way."

Stiarna emerged from the tree line then and stalked up the gangplank to board the ship.

"Is she going with us?" He pointed to Stiarna, who had perched on the very end of the bowsprit and was grooming herself.

"It's up to her." I shrugged. "It might be hard for a one-winged griffin to get by without a little help."

He looked at me then, his brow furrowed in that way that gave him three deep wrinkles between his dark eyes. "I think it's hard for anyone to get by without a little help."

Perhaps he was right, but I would never admit it.

The next morning, I braced myself against the railing behind the helm while the *Iron Duchess* trembled and rocked perilously. Beside me, Stiarna, whose wing was still bound and who had declined to disembark before we set sail, squawked and shuffled her feet.

Holding the wheel, Arun looked gleeful but also maybe a little nervous, which did little to calm my own nerves. Even so, we left the ground with a groan, the wind catching the sails and pulling them taut.

Grissall and Xalph sat nearby, playing a game of cards they'd found below deck, wholly unconcerned with the condition of the ship. Estrid and Erik stood near the bow, holding on to the foremast. I'd been worried that he wouldn't come or that I would have to go fetch him from Barepost again, but he hadn't said anything else after leaving the ship earlier. He held tight enough to the mast that the knuckles on his good hand were white with strain. Estrid looked pleased and kept glancing at our brother with a smile on her face. The first real smile I'd seen from her in a long time.

It wasn't until the ship cleared the treetops and came out on the other side of the veil that Beru and Aria emerged from below deck. Aria went to stand beside my sister, saying something that made both of them laugh. But Beru turned and found me watching him. I knew he was looking at the star, knew he was congratulating himself at finding Onen Suun's heir who would save the world. The world that Onen Suun himself died to protect.

I offered him a small, hesitant smile.

But I knew in my gut what the priestess would say. I wasn't a Suun—could not be a Suun. I was a Svand. And somehow, I would prove it.

And after that, I would take us home.

Continue reading this series, Legends of the Fallen with book 5, Breaking the Suun
books2read.com/u/bwjXOe

Grab the free prequel to the Legends of the Fallen series, Falling Suun here:
https://books2read.com/u/3R1ElD

Like the series Facebook page to stay up to date on all new releases
https://www.facebook.com/LegendsoftheFallen

ABOUT THE AUTHOR

J.A. Culican is a USA Today Bestselling author of the middle grade fantasy series Keeper of Dragons. Her first novel in the fictional series catapulted a trajectory of titles and awards, including top selling author on the USA Today bestsellers list and Amazon, and a rightfully earned spot as an international best seller. Additional accolades include Best Fantasy Book of 2016, Runner-up in Reality Bites Book Awards, and 1st place for Best Coming of Age Book from the Indie Book Awards.

J.A. Culican holds a master's degree in Special Education from Niagara University, in which she has been teaching special education for over 13 years. She is also the president of the autism awareness non-profit Puzzle Peace United. J.A. Culican resides in Southern New Jersey with her husband and four young children.

For more information about J.A. Culican, visit her website at: www.jaculican.com.

ABOUT THE AUTHOR

Cassidy studied English and Creative Writing at the University of North Carolina at Chapel Hill and won the Bill Hooks Award for Young Adult Fiction in 2007. She lives in beautiful North Carolina with her husband, two kids, two dogs, and one cat who thinks he's a dog.

For more information about Cassidy Taylor, visit her website at: http://cassidytaylor.net/

ACKNOWLEDGMENTS

Editor: Frankie Blooding
Cover Artist: Christian Bentulan
Formatting: Dragon Realm Press